FARTHING HALL

Fagg. Sir, there has been a great spattering of ink among these gentlemen.

Purden. Doubtless they have known great affairs.

Fagg. Nay, sir, 'tis all fantastick, I'll swear; so many silly toys and fables, out-moded fripperies, worse than your Grub Street gear.

Purden. Well, for my part, Master Fagg, I'll take an oath that Truth casts a shadow or two here as she does elsewhere. . . .

Act IV, Knighton's *Devil take the Hindmost.*

HUGH WALPOLE

AND

J.B. PRIESTLEY
FARTHING HALL

INTRODUCTION BY TOM PRIESTLEY

ALAN SUTTON PUBLISHING LIMITED

First published in 1929

First published in this edition in the United Kingdom in 1995
Alan Sutton Publishing Limited
Phoenix Mill · Far Thrupp · Stroud · Gloucestershire

British Library Cataloguing in Publication Data
A catalogue record for this book is available from the British Library.

ISBN 0-7509-1047-X

Cover picture: detail from Girl in an Interior *(Tate Gallery, London)*

Typeset in 10/11 Bembo.
Typesetting and origination by
Alan Sutton Publishing Limited.
Printed in Great Britain by
The Guernsey Press Company Limited,
Guernsey, Channel Islands.

INTRODUCTION

It was literature which brought Hugh Walpole and J.B. Priestley together. In 1925, Priestley, then not yet thirty, was invited by the publishers Messrs Jarrold to edit a series called 'These Diversions'. Naturally he approached Hugh Walpole, one of the leading popular novelists of the time, with twenty published books (mainly novels) already behind him; whereas Priestley, who was writing articles and working as a reader for John Lane, had published only five books (collections of essays or literary biographies). Walpole immediately invited Priestley to stay at Brackenburn, his home in the Lake District, to discuss the project. His diary tracks their relationship: 'Sept. 24. Arrived Priestley – a North-Country, no-nonsense-about-me, I-know-my-mind kind of little man. But I think I shall like & respect him. Sept. 25. I find Priestley very agreeable. He is cocksure and determined but has a great sense of humour about himself and his views on literature most strangely coincide with mine. Sept. 30. Priestley is certainly a very clever man . . . he . . . will go far.'

Walpole agreed to write on 'The Pleasures of Reading', which he set to and wrote in six days. Their friendship continued, though it was, as Priestley wrote in *Margin Released*, 'a friendship of opposites. He was always wildly anxious to please, whereas I have a talent, almost a genius, for displeasing all but those near to me. He was fond of making lists, of favourite people, books, experiences and so on, something I never did even as a schoolboy.' Yet they became, in his own words, 'close friends', and Walpole was to write in his diary: 'I've never had a writing man for a friend before who has been so close a companion. Henry James was too old, Conrad too mysterious, Swinnerton too untrustworthy, Bennett too egoistic – all good friends, but none of them with this humour and sweetness that Priestley has. A most lovable man.' Priestley wrote: 'Walpole's innocent warm vanity was better than my cool conceit. He had far more genuine humility than I had. He was more considerate, more generous, much kinder than I have ever been.'

During a visit to Walpole in June 1927, the two of them agreed to collaborate in a novel to be called *Farthing Hall*. 'The story was told in letters exchanged between a middle-aged scholar and an enthusiastic young man. Though I was neither middle-aged nor a scholar, this was the role I preferred, leaving eager youth and romance to Walpole,' wrote Priestley.

The idea for doing a book together was entirely Walpole's – a typical act of generosity. He knew Priestley wanted to write a substantial novel, but could not afford the time to write it with four children to support. Walpole then was a popular and successful novelist with a long and solid relationship with his publisher Macmillan, and so able to command a decent advance on royalties – exactly what Priestley needed to allow himself time to write his new long novel.

They started work together in September 1927 at Brackenburn; it was a collaboration which enhanced their friendship, as Walpole noted in his diary: 'Sept. 21. . . . it is delightful having Jack here – a friendship that does me all the good in the world because I respect so immensely his intelligence. Sept. 22. The book with Priestley moves. I have as expected a burning desire to get on with it. Sept. 26. Jack & I now moving at breakneck speed.' On 5 January 1928, Priestley wrote a letter to his stepmother in Bradford from College House, the house he rented in Church Hanborough, Oxfordshire: 'I am going up to London in a week's time to stay with Walpole so that we can finish our novel, *Farthing Hall*, together. I have just begun my new long novel, *The Good Companions*. It begins in the West Riding but wanders all over the place, is comic and deals with some people who run a pierrot troupe. You'll like it I think.'

The Good Companions was dedicated simply: 'To Hugh Walpole, for a friendship that has even triumphantly survived a collaboration'. Walpole returned the compliment when in 1933 he dedicated *Judith Paris* to J.B. Priestley.

It is well worth reflecting on the basis of this 'friendship of opposites'. Plainly there was a shared sense of humour and a relish for lively conversation. After a visit to Church Hanborough in 1928, Walpole wrote in his diary: 'Jane and Jack suit me exactly both in character and mind – splendid acquisitions for me. We talked a million to the clock;' and later, 'Of all the literary men I've known Jack Priestley is by far the best talker and he only when he's in the mood'. Priestley wrote of Walpole: 'He was a lively talker and had far more humour in private than his public appearances might suggest. He had known the authors I had missed and was full of stories about them.'

But beyond the talk and the laughter, they shared a deep love of literature and respect for their predecessors – the writers whose books they both read so avidly and whose footsteps they consciously followed. They shared a strong sense of tradition, as if they for the moment were carrying the baton in a relay race and should pass it on in turn to their successors. Though they lived and worked into the age of modernism, they were by temperament traditionalists; Priestley, however, was more experimental in his plays than has sometimes been appreciated.

Hugh Walpole was always a welcome visitor at the Priestleys' home, and is still remembered with affection as 'Uncle Hugh' by my sisters. He was godfather to two of them, but always brought presents for all five children, carefully chosen, some still cherished to this day. They remember him as large and pink, with a highish voice and an explosive and infectious laugh. In the summer of 1939, he suddenly turned up during breakfast at Billingham Manor, the Priestleys' house on the Isle of Wight; apparently he had been visiting the poet Alfred Noyes, and they had had such a heated argument about Joyce's *Ulysses* that he couldn't sleep and escaped first thing in the morning to take refuge with the Priestley family.

Walpole and Priestley carried on seeing each other when they found time; after a lunch late in 1939, Walpole wrote: 'I think I am fonder of him every time I see him. His growls and pessimism all come from liver. He must have one of the worst in the animal kingdom.' Priestley wrote: 'Now and then he might be over-excited, almost hysterical, probably because his diabetes was not under control. But most of the time . . . he was uproariously good company; I knew him for sixteen years, and have missed him for twenty.'

When, after Walpole's death on 1 June 1941, *The Times* printed a mean-spirited obituary, J.B. Priestley was among those who sprang to his old friend's defence, ending his letter: 'Finally your notice makes no mention of what was obvious to anybody who knew Walpole – namely that he really loved literature, old and new, and was always ready to risk being sneered and jeered at, if he felt he could call attention to good new work and help younger writers. . . . The world of contemporary English letters, I prophesy, will be much bleaker without Hugh Walpole.'

TOM PRIESTLEY

Telegram from
   MARK FRENCH
      of 20 Jermyn Street, London, W.

to

   ROBERT NEWLANDS
      of Peartree Lodge, Little Hurliford, Oxon.

Regret unable keep appointment. Letter explaining follows.   FRENCH.

Telegram from
   ROBERT NEWLANDS,
      Peartree Lodge, Little Hurliford, Oxon.

to

   MARK FRENCH,
      The Mitre, Oxford.

   Sorry lunch off. Explain later.   NEWLANDS.

IN THE TRAIN GOING NORTH.

MY DEAR BOB,

Forgive in the first place this shaky writing. You know my hand well
enough by now: the train turns it into something rich and strange. All
the same it's readable for anyone who understands me as well as you do.
But do you understand me, or will you after you hear of the crazy thing
that I'm now doing?

Well now, first for your scolding. I can just see you with your wrinkles
of savage disgust when you read my telegram. Or perhaps, horrible
thought, you never got it at all. I calculated that it ought to reach you
nicely before you started for Oxford, but I suppose that I should have
telephoned. I thought of that, of course, but I had awful visions of
Marjorie coming to the telephone, wanting to know, expostulating. 'Oh,
but you've *got* to come . . . Bob will be furious. He's given up all his
morning's work to go in to Oxford. . . .' So I funked it and wired. If it
didn't reach you in time, if you really sat at the Mitre and waited for me,
well then I can expect no mercy. I'm horribly ashamed. I'll stand all the
rough treatment that you can give me. But don't think that I've been
casual or selfishly forgetful. You know that I'm pretty good about
engagements. My past record ought to help me. This is exceptional.
Exceptional! By God, it's the maddest, craziest, wildest thing I've ever
done in all my life. And the worst of it is I'm not sorry − I'm not
repentant. I'm excited, Robert, as I've never been before. Excited, yes,
and happy! It's the first adventure I've ever had, the adventure you've
always been wanting me to have, the adventure that you're for ever
insisting I *must* have. And now I've taken you at your word. On your
own head be it! Now listen!

Last night I should have dined with Frank Carter, you know, the fellow
who wants to paint like Gauguin and ends in pictures like Ambrose
McEvoy's. Nice fellow all the same. I was just dressing when he
telephoned that his wife had come back a day earlier from Bournemouth
and he'd got to stay in. Thank God, says I, I'm not married, and continue
to dress. It was rather nice to have an evening suddenly free. What should
I do? Go to bed with a novel and a cutlet? Play bridge at the
Sandringham? Or the theatre? Certainly the theatre. You know that I'm
still a child where the theatre is concerned. I've the regular oranges-and-
sawdust temperament. I'm your country cousin the moment the lights go

down and the curtain goes up. And there was a gorgeous melodrama I hadn't seen. You share that cult with me. Your complaint is there aren't enough good ones. Well, there was the one we'd been talking about only last week, *The Man with Green Eyes*. The very thought of it hastened me over my dressing. I rushed out, got a taxi, had a sandwich at the Sandringham, and half an hour later was in the fourth row of the stalls. The first Act was glorious. It was a packed house (I was lucky to get a returned seat). The thing opened in exactly the right way. An empty room with a clock ticking and a canary in a cage (watch the canary!). Fellow in evening dress followed by a woman in one of those tight-fitting silver dresses making her look like a mermaid. Fearful row. Man loses his temper, lady hers. Lady accuses him of infidelity, man horribly bored. Man strangles lady. Man departs out of window. After he's gone cheery old red-faced boy, hitherto hidden in arm-chair, is discovered, witness of everything. Smiles, hums a tune, drags lady into adjoining room. Goes to canary and gives it a piece of sugar à la Fosco – and so on, and so on. First Act keeps it up splendidly. Curtain goes down on sudden casual entrance of lady, silver mermaid exactly like the lady who has been murdered. . . . Everyone staggered except the canary.

This was fine. I thought I'd go out and have a drink. I was about to move when I noticed the girl sitting next to me. Now you know how you're always accusing me of noticing women with a painter's eye but never with a human one. How many times you've bored and irritated me with this, irritated me because I suppose there's some truth in it. Not that you want me to be romantic in sober truth; you'd be disgusted, I'm sure. This time you've got your revenge. It was not that she was so beautiful. In fact now I can't really describe her to you. I don't know even that I want to try. She was dark, slim, young, lovely eyes (those I can swear to), very simply dressed. What was it? What is it ever? What happened to me at that moment? I'm none of your damned modern novelists. I only know that I sat there in my seat, the melodrama forgotten, my heart beating like a dinner-gong. She hadn't looked at me. She was staring in front of her. I could see that her thoughts were a thousand miles away. I could see more as I snatched furtive glances at her. She was unhappy. She was struggling with herself about something, something to her of the deepest, most serious importance. Now I can see you smile, that beastly caustic, cynical smile of yours. 'Ha! ha! Caught at last, my young friend!' Yes, I'm caught, hopelessly, desperately. Thank God for it!

Looking at her I saw that on the other side of her was sitting a young fellow, handsome in a loose chinless way, with the chalk-and-paste countenance of one to whom sleep's a stranger and drink a tyrannous friend. A shiftier, weaker young idiot even you, investigator of lost human causes, never set eyes on. They were together, but not, it seemed,

on speaking terms. He sat beside her, restless, uneasy, playing
chuckpenny, I should fancy, with the remains of a conscience. He at last
muttered something to her and shuffled his way out. After he'd gone she
suddenly sighed and I saw her tighten her two hands together as though
she were at the very limit of endurance. At the same moment she
dropped her programme. I bent down and picked it up for her. She
smiled at me and thanked me. She has the softest, gentlest voice . . . but
no, you don't deserve my ecstasies. I thought then that I might make a
venture. I asked her whether she liked the play. Daring of me, wasn't it?
You know my diffidence; on this occasion all my laws were broken. She
was frightened at my speaking to her but she answered me — vaguely, at
random. Had her thoughts not been so desperately engaged elsewhere
she'd have snubbed me perhaps. As it was she scarcely knew that she was
talking to me. We talked a little, I so excited that I could scarcely speak.
We talked of the theatre, plays, the weather. Her answers were short and
most certainly not encouraging, but so gentle, so shy, so young (she
wasn't, I fancied, a day more than nineteen), that I felt, as the minutes
went by, that I longed to protect her, to help her, to tell her that I'd do
anything for her. . . . Idiocy. Maybe. Heaven be praised I'm an idiot at
last.

But the minutes were passing. The chinless oaf (was he brother,
husband, friend, what?) would be returning. My tongue in my stomach,
I asked her whether she lived in London. 'No,' she said, realising me
suddenly then, I think, and definitely withdrawing. But I plunged once
more. Was she staying in London? Then she was definitely frightened.
She said 'No' quickly. She was leaving Euston for the North to-morrow
by the morning express. As she said it I could see that she would speak
no more, but at the same time I fancied — was it madness? was it only
fancy? I have tortured myself a thousand times since then with the
question — that she told me that deliberately, or perhaps not me exactly —
anyone who was near, who would help her for a moment to seem not so
utterly alone and helpless. . . . Well, a moment later the oaf returned, the
curtain went up. I saw, of course, no more of the melodrama. I was aware
only that I was sitting next to her, that my knee touched her dress, that
my hand was close to hers.

And then — Oh Robert, the agony of it — suddenly they got up and
went. The theatre was in pitch darkness at the time. They were firing
revolvers on the stage. I could hear people mutter impatiently as they
passed out. I had a crazy instinct to get up and follow them. But the
moment passed. I waited. It was too late.

As soon as the second Act was over I went out and home. I thought it
was a momentary madness. I sat in my room and drank whiskies and
sodas. I looked at my Segonzac — you know, the one of the old peasant in

the field – and said, 'Well, that's over, old boy. Dashed pretty girl. *That's* over.' But it wasn't. Not a bit of it. I went to bed, and as soon as the lights were out she was there, there standing beside my bed. Her dark eyes, her quiet voice, her childish unhappiness and distress. . . . Robert, I knew then in those hours that night at last what love was. Yes, laugh as much as you like, let this adventure have the most ludicrous ending you please, or, as is more likely, no ending at all, I know now what love is. I can never be ignorant again.

In the morning I knew exactly what I was going to do. I was going up to Euston to see whether she were there. I thought of you and Oxford. My dear old boy, you and Oxford were a million miles away.

With a bag I went to Euston. I got a ticket for Carlisle on the chance – moving all this time blindly like a man dreaming, but obstinately as though nothing in the world was going to stop me. I sent a telegram to you. I walked up the platform looking into every compartment. No sign of her. Five minutes before the train was due to start she appeared, alone, hurrying, in a little grey fur hat and coat. She didn't see me. Of course she wouldn't recognise me. She got into a first-class with three other women, I into the compartment next to hers. And so here we are. We've just passed Rugby and I shall post this at Crewe. Where she goes I go. I'll know her and help her. Yes, if I lose the world, the arts, and all my silly old ambitions in doing so. Nothing – *nothing*, you hear, Robert – shall stop me. Write to Jermyn Street; letters will be forwarded when I know an address. Be patient with me. I've woken up to real life at last.

Yours ever,
MARK.

PEARTREE LODGE,
LITTLE HURLIFORD,
OXON.

MY DEAR MARK,

It's a miracle that I can write at all. For the last two days I have been leading the life of an hotel manager. I have been sending and receiving telegrams, watching cars squeeze in and out of the garage here, running up and down stairs carrying things, and talking at the top of my voice. If this letter is still at the top of my voice, you must forgive me. I am not myself. *The Chimera of Romanticism* – which you will kindly remember is the name of the critical masterpiece I came here to write – has receded into a tiny point of light, somewhere beyond Sirius. I cannot believe in the existence of the chapters already done or the notebooks on my desk. It belongs to another life, before the deluge. But I must tell you about the deluge. Let me begin at the beginning.

I wired to you at the Mitre yesterday morning to say that our lunch was off. Marjorie insisted on my staying here to play host. Apparently you were not there, for the wire you sent me, which arrived after mine had gone, was handed in at Euston. I was not surprised when it came, because by that time I had come to the conclusion that the last gleams of reason were fading from the world, that chaos had come again. To be exact, chaos arrived here at about eleven yesterday morning, when there descended upon us, out of that blue which hides so many horrors, a car full of people and luggage. It was Mrs Masham and her retinue. Do you know the Masham? She is a very rich, middle-aged widow, tall and stout, with the square face, slab of forehead, and upstanding grey hair of an old-fashioned German pianist; and she writes a little and talks for ever. She is one of those women whose minds exist in a strange mid-air of nebulous profundities: she deals in Higher Thought and New Rhythm and the Infinite Consciousness and the Upward Way, and she liberally sprinkles her talk with the names of philosophers and poets she has never read, of pictures she has never seen, and music she has never heard. The result is that she always seems to be discussing the affairs of some other and quite different planet. You hear her voice going maddeningly on and on, and your mind rushes forward time after time to grasp something, only to find that it is clutching empty air. She herself, however, is not nebulous but solid enough. She is twelve stone or so of greed, vanity and selfishness, having been hopelessly spoilt by her money and a crowd of silly friends and admirers. As soon as her husband died (he left her some vast emporium or factory), she turned to Higher Thought and the New Rhythm as some women turn to good works and others to bridge and cocktails. Then she produced a treatise on nothing called *The Golden Way*, and an even more atrocious thing, an attempt at fiction, called *The New Dawn*, and both these works, having been advertised as if they were patent medicines, have been sold by the tens of thousand among the half-baked. Since then she has never stopped talking. She is talking here now: her voice rolls in through my study window. But what is she doing here? There shall be no secrets between us. The truth is, then, the painful truth, that your friend, Marjorie Newlands – my wife, Marjorie Newlands – invited her.

We met her at the Chillingfords' last winter. I disliked her at sight (we men, Mark, may be unreasonable, but we have our intuitions), but, to my surprise, Marjorie didn't. She found something in her – and to this day I don't know exactly what – to pity and to admire. Since then they have met twice, purely by accident, I think, and each time Marjorie has murmured that 'there is something about poor Mrs Masham, you know——'; and each time I have told her that I don't know. Marjorie, of course, is not duped by the woman's nebulous chatter: I never knew her to be taken in by claptrap of that kind; but she insists that she finds her interesting and will not agree with me that the Masham is simply a very vain, selfish and rather vulgar woman. Little did I dream that Marjorie had gone to the length of inviting the woman here. It was, to be sure, one of those vague, general come-down-anytimes that are usually understood to mean nothing. She might have known, though, that the Masham, who seems to be delighted with her (as well she might be), would take her at her word whenever it happened to be convenient. And the trouble is that Marjorie doesn't mind, seems quite pleased. She refuses to give them any hint about going on the plea that I am busy with my book (and I was just getting into my stride); and tells me that I can work quite well with them here or – with the usual alternative reason that the feminine mind produces – that I need a rest. As if I could either work or rest with that woman here! Moreover, she is not alone. There is a secretary-companion, Miss Banks, a watery-looking female who seems to stare at the world through a slight mist, and whose duty it is in talk to remind her employer of her triumphs. ('*And* the presentation, Mrs Masham! Don't forget that!') But I think her real opinion of the Masham would be worth hearing. But we have not only the Banks but also the brays. They proceed from a young imbecile of a nephew who seems to be acting as Mrs Masham's chauffeur. He has just returned from the Riviera, and when he is not talking about it he relapses into an interminable series of yawns. I suspect that he is a very minor character that was left over when some Russian comedy was put together. Marjorie pretends to no affection for this pair, but shows no signs of losing her interest in Mrs Masham herself, who, I suspect, grossly flatters her when they are alone together. I think I know the line of approach. Marjorie can't resist anybody who tells her that she can be of some special use, and that there is something unusually fine about the atmosphere she has created in her home. (And I suppose that I can probably be flattered far more easily and grossly: I have no illusions there.) But isn't it odd? The woman is a horror. I can't understand Marjorie.

But there you are. You go marching along with a woman, keeping in step down all manner of queer roads – then suddenly up pops a Mrs Masham or some other absurdity – and you find that you are staring at one another and screaming across a gulf. And now, with so much steam let off, I feel better.

Yours ever,
ROBERT.

P.S. – Don't come here till I give the word, then you and Marjorie and I (delightfully Masham-less) will sit in the garden, eating pears and watching these old stone walls flushing to a delicate pink in the sunlight.

STATION HOTEL,
KESWICK.

MY DEAR BOB,

There hasn't been time for me to have a letter from you yet, but I wish
there had. I feel absurdly, ridiculously lonely. For one of England's best
painters, self-reliant, self-confident, egoist and flâneur – see advertisements
– this feeling that I have this evening sitting in the smoky hotel reading-
room, the windows tear-stained with the eternally histrionic weather, the
tables littered with *Tatlers* and motor journals, the floor littered with aged
ladies a-playing at Patience – Oh, why am I here, why are you there? No,
but of course I know why I'm here. I will continue my dramatic and
'Ancient Mariner'-like story, only don't expect anything *very* dramatic
this time. To-day I've drawn blank. To-morrow I shall no doubt do the
same. I was never, as you know, the most patient of mortals.

My last letter left off with myself in the train passing Rugby, and my
beloved, my adored one, my beautiful stranger, my Elegant Unknown
sitting in the very next compartment all unwitting the fate in store for
her (see *The Man with Green Eyes*). Well, the Lord knows how many
immortal hours I sat in that damned compartment. When the man came
along tinkling the luncheon bell, 'Now surely,' says I, 'my darling will
want something to eat,' but my darling didn't want anything of the sort.
She's made, no doubt, of some heavenly substance that sneers at chops
and shudders before the homely cabbage. Not so I. I am, in spite of
immortal longings and my divine gift, equipped with gullet, stomach and
all complete. I sat there growing hungrier and hungrier, but never daring
to move lest we should stop at some station and she get out there. My
compartment reeked of the tobacco of my neighbours; I had bought, in a
kind of blind indifference at Euston, a bunch of magazines. And what
magazines! I open the first and there is a story of beautiful unknown girl
pursued by reckless lover over wastes of ice and snow. My own story! I
push a little further. Another story of same beautiful unknown girl
pursued by same lover through horrid jungles of Chicago. My story
again. Open another magazine, start another story. Same beautiful
unknown pursued by same lover, this time through the thick herbage of
Central Africa! Good God! Am I then only one of a vast commonplace
herd? I who thought I was unique in this amazing never-before-known
adventure! Another slap to my poor pride. And the train goes on and on.

We never stop. I might just as well have had my fragment of blue-eyed turbot and slab of horse-bred beef. The rain poured, the pipes gurgled (private briars, I mean); I want to sleep, I dare not. I long to walk down the corridor and peep at her. For some strange Freudian reason I dare not.

Then at last with a jerk and a grunt we stopped. Some horrid place like Wigan. I got out and watched the platform. I even walked casually past her compartment feeling myself guilty of some secret sin. There she was, curled up in her corner, so sweet, so young, so innocent. . . . Oh Robert, wasn't my lunchless, smoky journey worth it a thousand times over? Indeed and indeed it was. Well, I must cut this short or you'll never read to the end of it. We stopped now at every little station. The country now was opening out into wide naked slopes and little stone walls. The air, when I sniffed any of it, was fresh and clean, and the rain as smugly self-satisfied as any I've ever beheld. It grew darker and colder, and I hungrier and hungrier. We stopped again. This time Penrith. I felt somehow that this was our crisis — and it was! There she was stepping on to the platform, and there was I, bag in hand, slipping after her. She didn't leave the station. She asked no questions of the porter. She was going on somewhere else and she knew all about the trains. She'd done this journey before.

I followed her down the platform, sharp turn to the left, saw her put her bag into the first-class compartment of a little lonely, self-conscious train dedicated to Keswick. So that was where she was bound! Keswick of the Lakes, Southey and Coleridge, lead pencils and the Lodore trickle. I've been there before. Years ago. You remember I told you once how we sat on the side of a mountain and the rain ran into our hard-boiled eggs and out at our boots! Yes, well, Keswick it was once more to be! She meanwhile had gone off to the ladies' cloak-room. There was half an hour to wait. This time I placed my bag in the same compartment exactly opposite to hers, faint-heart no longer. The divine moment came. I was sitting opposite to her. The little train had started.

Again that dazzling, choking, fiery sensation had seized me. Hadn't I just been reading about that very same sensation in those cursed magazines? Yes, but these emotions were my own — my very, very own — and new to me, so new that they didn't seem to belong to me at all. I looked at her, and looked and looked. I could analyse a little now the charm that she had for me. She is beautiful. I think that even you, unromantic cynic that you are, would agree to that. Her colour is lovely, fresh and delicate in its bloom, pale but not too pale, flushed with life that is ignorant but eager and has no knowledge yet of its charm. She is modest, I swear, and gentle and kindly. Brave and honest. She can laugh, too, I know, when some of this trouble that is hemming her in is past.

And it *shall* pass if I know anything of determination in my heart. She took a book out of her bag and began to read. What do you think it was? *Pride and Prejudice*! She had read about a quarter of it. I knew just the point that she had reached. Suddenly she smiled. Oh, how happy I was to see that even for a moment she could forget her troubles. I could swear she was smiling over Mr Collins' letter. I couldn't resist it, I leaned forward and said as gently as possible: 'Mr Collins is splendid, isn't he?'

She knew me – at once. The sound of my voice, the way that I asked the question. She gave me a look. She blushed. I could see that she was determined to be the grand woman of the world.

'Yes,' she said stiffly. 'He is very amusing.'

I dared again. 'We sat next one another at the theatre last night.'

'Yes. I think we did.'

'An odd coincidence,' I murmured.

She didn't reply to that at all, but sat with her eyes deep in the book. And then, miserable, awkward coward that I am, I didn't dare another word! For the next half-hour there we sat in a miserable silence – and now I hadn't even the happy pleasure of her adorable nose, her bewitching mouth.

We were at Keswick. Some kind of man – a rough servant kind of person, chauffeur *in rure* I should imagine – was waiting for her. She had no heavy luggage. Only her suit-case. I followed after them, saw her through the dusk climb into a very rustic-looking motor car, and she was gone.

Nothing for me to do but find a room in the Station Hotel here. Nothing for me to do but sleep and eat (both things miraculously but most unromantically I'm able to do). That was last night. To-day I've searched Keswick. Not a sign of her, of course. I've asked cautious questions. But what have I to go on? Nothing except the clothes, the country chauffeur, the shabby ancient car. Nevertheless she can't be so far away. Keswick's her station. That was her own family's servant. That I'll swear. She belongs near here, and I'll find her if I have to drain the district through a sieve. Meanwhile I'm lonely and restless. *Hinc illae lacrymae.* Hence this long letter to you. And you'll get more of them. I've no one in the world but yourself to confide in – you, you grumpy, disillusioned, sarcastic, but marvellously understanding devil.

Oh Robert, where is she? Who is she? What is she? Is she married or single? Why is she so unhappy? But she did smile over Mr Collins, didn't she?

Your affectionate
MARK.

PEARTREE LODGE,
LITTLE HURLIFORD,
OXON.

MY DEAR MARK,

Your two bombshells received and duly exploded. I am not sure yet whether your adventure, this chasing of a pretty girl you don't know across England, is one of gallantry or chivalry. If it turns out to be an odd mixture of both, you may depend upon it that you're in love. But of course you are already depending upon it. Fortunately, you are not badly off where you are. If you never see the girl again, or if you discover that she is engaged to some Cumberland stripling at present in the Sudan but shortly arriving on leave and in a new two-seater, or if you make her acquaintance only to find that she is all giggles and stupidity, then at least there are any number of mountains to climb, and you can sweat and tire yourself into good sense again. Indeed, I suggest you try a walk to the top of Great Gable before you make any other move. See what she looks like from Great Gable. I warn you, though, that she probably adores the unpleasant young man who was with her at the theatre, and that he probably isn't unpleasant at all. In fact, I could go on warning you all day — it's an ideal occupation, this warning, for a vain man with nothing much to do — but modesty and friendship must break in somewhere. So I will simply say that I really know nothing whatever about it and that I am eagerly awaiting more news.

It's more than likely that in a day or two you will either be scrambling cheerfully about the fells (which will be turning into gold the first fine morning, with the distant peaks just breathed upon the sky, all smoky and opalescent), or taking the train back to Jermyn Street, that, in short, you will be a chick shrugging itself out of the broken shell of romance. Nevertheless, I say, you have had your journey. That is what I envy you, that absurd train journey, flashing north so fantastically, staring out of your window and watching the inns turn themselves into castles and the windmills into giants. I have always felt that that is the spirit in which long train journeys were meant to be undertaken: a dash for love or war, sudden death or heart's desire. So don't fret if reality, which includes so many silly girls with faces too good for 'em and so many lads who change their minds after every shower of rain, blows out all the coloured lights at the other end. You have had your journey. The thought of it makes me feel old. There are no more such journeys for me.

I told Marjorie about your adventure. I was certain that she would at once either denounce your fair unknown (and with her your daft quest and everything) or declare that she is the very girl for you, though I can't see myself that there is a pin's worth of evidence for one judgment or the other. And I was right.

'I do hope Mark gets to know her,' she said, thoughtfully, busy planning where you were both to live and what we should give you for a wedding present. 'I hope he doesn't run away. She seems the very girl for him.' There was bright defiance in her eye when she said that.

'My dear,' I replied, as heavy as a husband in a play, 'you don't know anything about the girl except that she's pretty and modest and lives somewhere near Keswick and enjoys Jane Austen.' I had given her these details, and now that I mentioned them again, they did seem quite a good deal to know about a person.

'I know more than that,' she said, 'and so do you. You're pretending to be stupid. I like the sound of her. I knew something was going to happen to Mark very soon. I was talking about him only last night to Hilda Masham, who's promised to buy some of his work.'

Let me confess it. This annoyed me, and I went sulking away. Your adventure had sent us skimming back – for you know how Marjorie lights up at such things – to what I must sadly call the pre-Masham period, the golden age. And now it is *Hilda* Masham. She is still here, and I have come to loathe the sight of her greasy slab of forehead, her little greedy eyes, and her big loose mouth, out of which comes a perpetual stream of words she does not understand. The imbecile Russian-comedy nephew, I am glad to say, departed yesterday, taking the Masham car with him. He kept up his idiotic part to the very end. He muttered something about the Corniche, gave two yawns, and was gone. Miss Banks, the secretary-companion, remains, and has looked more watery than ever these last two or three days. It is obvious that the Masham gives her a very bad time, and I suspect she has been worse than usual since they arrived here. Behind Miss Banks' mechanical gush, her pale near-sighted eyes and faintly streaming face, there is a spirit not yet entirely subdued by incessant typewriting and telephoning, fetching and carrying, and all the simpering slavery of paid companionship. (Probably the amount of courage and determination needed by Miss Banks to keep smiling and smiling and turning the other cheek would suffice, in a robust male, to conquer one of the Central American republics.) Something happened in the drawing-room last night just after dinner and before I joined them, a last stamp of the Masham flat heel, that left Miss Banks hurt and vaguely rebellious. I believe that Marjorie herself was rather shocked, but she has probably come to the conclusion since that it only means that her Hilda

Masham will need even more attention than she imagined, a deeper and more thorough saturation in the Marjorie atmosphere. (For I know what Marjorie's after, where her little vanities lie.) Meanwhile, Miss Banks, resentment gleaming faintly through her usual mistiness, is not to my eye quite the docile creature she was four days ago. And if I spy the tiniest flame, I shall tiptoe up and drop upon it the oil of smooth false words. I made a beginning this morning by asking her casually about former employers. Were they pleasant or unpleasant? Several of them, she told me proudly, were nice, very nice, 'real ladies.'

'And that,' she added, lowering her voice, 'makes such a difference, such a difference.'

'Yes,' I agreed, eyeing her thoughtfully. 'It must make a great difference.' And we stared at one another for a moment. Then she pursed up her foolish mouth, nodded rather severely, and went moistly away. Poor Miss Banks!

I cannot be downright rude to this Masham woman in my own house, but I never came nearer to being rude to any guest. The trouble is, she is so insensitive. Quiet snubs fall unheeded to the ground like so many snowflakes. Irony she simply does not understand. It is Marjorie – who does understand, confound it! – who receives these shafts on her own target, and sends back a few arrows from time to time, with an unerring eye for the joints in my armour; while this gross foolish female sprawls and blathers between us without once guessing what is happening. And, to give the Masham her due, she is perfectly good-humoured towards me, for ever turning up smiling. She has certain catchwords and pet phrases that nearly drive me cursing from the table. Thus, when four or five of the half-witted are exchanging their bosh, she calls this 'a gathering'; and we have, it seems, the making of 'a gathering' here. (When she said this, Marjorie all but laughed out loud at the sight of my face. I fancy that Marjorie, whom some imp of mischief is inspiring, encourages her, with one eye on me.) Then some things are 'helpful' and others are 'astralised,' and some people 'have understanding' and are finding (for we are all seeking, it seems) 'the Way.' This goes on at every meal. Add to it remarks about a range of authors, from Edward Carpenter, who writes as if he were Whitman's maiden aunt, to one Ralph Waldo Trine, who would seem to write as if he were addressing a company of blancmanges. Then add to this, gross self-complacency, egoism, vulgarity and snobbery, and you may guess what I suffer. The *Chimera* cannot be touched, for I am too irritated to settle down to it again. For the last two days I have dropped hints about going, but Marjorie promptly counters by pressing the woman to stay.

That should tell you something. You have probably been thinking that I must be losing my sense of proportion to be so angry about a silly visitor. But the Masham, you see, is more than that: the malicious gods steered her in here; she is the apple of discord. I do not believe for a moment that Marjorie really cares tuppence about the woman. We do not talk a great deal about this business, but we have only to exchange a word or two for me to hear ominous rumbles and crackings beneath our feet. The arrival of Mrs Masham has only dragged into the light certain fundamental differences in our respective attitudes that we have pretended for the past year or two to ignore. I had to leave Oxford so that I could write the *Chimera*, the book that has been tantalising me for years, in peace, and this was obviously the place. Marjorie was as enthusiastic about it as I was, but she won't realise that some things would have to be given up. I don't believe that the feminine mind can ever grasp the fact that you cannot have your cake and eat it too. But no more of this. Let me have your news.

Yours,

ROBERT.

STATION HOTEL,
KESWICK.

MY DEAR BOB,

I have, thank the Lord, had two letters from you now and in a day or two I'll answer them fully. I don't feel nearly so alone now — partly because of your letters, and partly — but you shall hear.

After your second letter this morning I was so instantly swung into the middle of your affairs, and you and Marjorie both seemed so close to me, that I intended to sit down and write a long screed — all about YOU! Moreover, I've been here, there, three days now and, until this afternoon, had drawn completely blank. Add to that that it's rained almost without cessation. The country — although I've seen scarcely any of it — is green blotting-paper, and Keswick, until this same glorious afternoon, had seemed to me like a kennel for mongrels. I did find a book-shop, Chaplin's by name, with some good books in it too. And that same book-shop — as you shall in a moment hear — is written like Mary's Calais for ever on my heart, although for quite different reasons. I purchased Coleridge's *Biographia Literaria*, Clough's Poems, Buchan's *Midwinter*, and *The Woman in White*, and ought to have settled down. But no, I couldn't. I was haunted, and found myself starting out again and again into the rain, splashing through the streets, peering about me like an amateur detective, even on one occasion hiring a motor and dismally twisting into Borrowdale and splashing to Grasmere. All of no avail. She'd been keeping indoors, I don't doubt, and small blame to her.

The odd thing is that I haven't had the slightest intention of giving the thing up. Something seems to have held me here. As a rule, if there isn't an instant response I'm off and away. Whether it's picture or book or friend. But something has seemed to tell me that if I don't hold on this time I'm missing the chance of my life — and that, I believe, is true.

Yesterday all the same I had a fit of the blues. I had your first letter, but neither you nor Marjorie seemed to be especially interested in my adventure. Isn't it by the way rather unlike Marjorie to take up the kind of woman you so caustically describe? Are you sure you've got her correctly? I know what you are when you take a dislike to someone on sight. Marjorie's a fairly sound judge. I can feel your irritation bubbling under your words until I'm almost nervous of some precipitate move on your part. You can be as impatient as I, you know.

Well, I sat in this hotel (very decent place, by the way, in ordinary circumstances) listening to the old ladies' cackle and the rain and a distant (but not distant enough) loud speaker. I tried Coleridge, and it was like searching for sixpence inside a Christmas pudding, Clough, and it was always just going to be good poetry and never quite was, and Buchan, and found I remembered the tale too clearly. I went to bed in a vile temper, and as has been the case every night since I met her, so soon as I turned the lights out there she was, just out of my reach but giving me, so it seemed to me, some kind of a message. I couldn't sleep, got up, went out, walked the naked streets shining after the rain, wondered *what* had happened to me. I, who have hitherto lived only to be a good painter – and now if Gabriel had swung down from the church steeple and offered me to paint like El Greco or find my lady, I'd have chosen the second without a moment's hesitation. Next morning (*this* morning as ever was) I was tired and cross and, I think, a little off my head. There was your second letter to restore me, and it *did* do me all the good in the world. You and Marjorie seemed so sane and real, and you made that old woman and her crew so living to me that I could have sat down there and then and painted them all. I did sit down to begin a letter to you and – fell fast asleep! I slept until luncheon like one of God's chosen, dreamlessly, painlessly, and I woke with an odd certainty that this adventure of mine would shortly take a good turn.

After lunch I went down to Chaplin's to get another book or two. It wasn't raining for a miracle, the air was fresh and clear, people were busy and happy about the streets. I was standing just inside the door, Chaplin beside me showing me an edition of Southey's *Doctor*. Suddenly the little shop was transmuted. 'Why, there's the sun!' I cried, looked through the door, and, walking up the street swiftly, looking neither to right nor left, were my girl and my chinless young man!

As they passed the door I touched Chaplin's arm.

'Who is that lady?' I asked him as quietly as you please. 'I've seen her somewhere in London.'

He looked, then casually, having no knowledge of course that he was opening to me the gates of Paradise: 'Oh, that's Miss Rossett – Miss Jean Rossett and her brother.'

'Do they live in Keswick?' I asked casually, turning the pages of *The Doctor*.

'No. They live with their father up Garrowdale. Farthing Hall, that's the place; Mr Rossett's people have been there for generations. Queer old house. Deserted part of the valley too. I wouldn't care to live there myself.'

'Oh yes,' I said. 'Is that all of the family?'

'There's Mr Rossett's sister. Mrs Rossett's been dead these ten years. Odd gentleman, Mr Rossett.'

'Odd?' I asked.

'Unusual. Not like other people.'

He turned away to attend to some customer. I had my facts, though, all I wanted, and the queer thing was that the names, Garrowdale, Rossett, Farthing Hall, were stamped on my brain from my first hearing of them as though I'd known them all my life.

And Jean. Jean, Jean, Jean! Unmarried. The darling – didn't I know that she must be?

No more now, Robert. My head's buzzing with plans. Farthing Hall shall open its doors to me and reveal its secrets before you've expelled Mrs Masham from your Eden – and that day is not, I fancy from your last letter, long distant.

My love to Marjorie.

Yours,

MARK.

PEARTREE LODGE,
LITTLE HURLIFORD,
OXON.

MY DEAR MARK,

Your letter came by the afternoon post. I received it just as I was setting out for the station. No, Mrs Masham has not gone yet, but Miss Banks has. I was so pleased with her that I insisted upon taking her down to the station and making a pleasant little fuss. She was moister than ever, but she held her head high. It all happened at tea, which we had in the garden, the afternoon being quite warm, one of those luscious golden September afternoons that are like ripe fruit. I think I told you that Miss Banks has been rebellious lately. I imagine that the Masham has been anything but 'understanding' or 'helpful' these last two days, and this morning she was quite obviously out of humour, and I caught her snapping at poor Miss Banks like a great fat pike. (The whole house jangles with nerves and strained tempers: we go fretting and wrangling, in and out of the yellow sunlight, so many pariah dogs.) At tea we had the ever-welcome scene of the worm turning. I won't worry you with the details of the row, which had something to do with a subscription to a certain society. Miss Banks produced a letter she had written, forwarding the subscription or donation, and gave it to Mrs Masham to read and sign. Mrs Masham screeched at the sight of it, flung down the letter, and swore she had never promised to give the society a penny.

'Really, Miss Banks,' she cried, 'I can't think what you mean by writing like this without any order from me. I never promised to give these people anything. How can you? I'm more and more surprised at you. You're simply beginning to forget yourself.'

'But – but,' Miss Banks stammered, 'you promised to give them twenty-five pounds, and told me to remind you. I remember quite well, indeed I do. You promised.'

'I did nothing of the kind.' The Masham was screaming now. 'How dare you say such a thing!'

This seemed the moment to put a plate of tomato sandwiches under her nose, and this I promptly did, asking her to have one in a loud cheerful voice.

Miss Banks, shaking all over, fumbled in the gigantic handbag she carries with her, and produced a diary. 'I – I – made a note of it here at the time,' she faltered, holding out the diary. 'I distinctly remember.'

The Masham pushed aside the proffered diary. 'I don't wish to look at it.' She gave another push, and the diary fell out of Miss Banks' hand and dropped neatly upon a plate of bread and butter. 'I know very well what I said and what I didn't say,' the Masham screamed away. 'You're simply not telling me the truth, Miss Banks. I don't know what's come over you.'

This was too much for Miss Banks, who had grabbed the diary again only to find that a slice of bread and butter was sticking to it. She put them both down now, drew herself up, her head all a-tremble, and then sent the whole edifice of genteel slavery crashing to the ground. 'To think – to think – ' she began, spluttering. And then, shrill and defiant: 'Oh, you vulgar, vulgar woman! To talk to me like that! I've never been treated like this before, never, never! To think I should have left Lady Lofterhouse for this! An ignorant upstart!'

'A what!' You should have heard the Masham scream. I thought her eyes were about to pop out of her head.

Miss Banks' head was now trembling more violently than ever and she seemed not merely moist but wet. But she stuck to her guns, and fired the biggest of them again for a parting shot. 'I said an ignorant upstart,' she cried. Then she turned away, walked forward a few paces, stopped and looked back. 'I leave at once, this afternoon.' This she gave out with great dignity, but it was her last effort. She turned away again, and promptly burst into tears.

An hour later I was at the station with her. The poor woman was still trembling, still faintly streaming and misty, and I have no doubt that her agitation will set the next few weeks quivering for her. Nevertheless her exit was heroic, and I would have liked to have shouted a few hexameters in her praise and to have clashed a cymbal and sounded a flourish as her train went out. She had more handbags and bangles than any three human beings have the right to carry, but unlike two out of every three of our fellow-creatures she had just succeeded in rising to the very height of her courage, standing tiptoe on the last inch, and in saving her soul. If you do not spare a moment from the contemplation of your mountain beauty, or rather the music-and-moonshine image of her, to salute Miss Banks, then I hope you never set foot in Farthing Hall.

To-night Marjorie and I dined alone. Mrs Masham, it seems, retired to her room shortly after tea, collapsing like many another tyrant who has heard a shot or two in the palace yard. According to Marjorie, who spoke very briefly about it, the woman feels really hurt because she had done a great deal for Miss Banks, who therefore becomes the usual monster of ingratitude. There may be some truth in this. I don't know. Marjorie and I never discussed the matter, never even referred to the scene in the garden, which is one reason why I am boring you with it, for I have to talk about it to somebody. Indeed we said very little during dinner – a sombre and taciturn pair, passing the salt to one another across a chasm. Marjorie remained long enough after coffee to smoke a cigarette, which for once she contrived to turn into an uncompanionable proceeding, and then quietly withdrew, after giving me one long level glance. It is very curious. All the bright mischief has died out of her these last two days, and now I rather wish it was back again. I like the human comedy and flatter myself that I am sufficiently detached to enjoy even my own part in it, but somehow these early autumn evenings, with their hints of decay and their greying empty skies, provide a background that is too disturbing, out of key with the comedy itself, so that you want somebody else with you as audience. Give me the fragrance and moonshine of summer, the glittering night sky and cosy interiors of winter, and I can lounge in the empty stalls and perfectly enjoy the show of this life. But at this season it's too lonely being the detached observer. Hence – my dear Mark – these letters and their storms in the tea-cup.

Meanwhile, you seem to be on the point of walking into a German romance of the 'thirties. Garrowdale, which I visited years ago, is rather like that, an astonishing place concocted out of an old engraving, the frontispiece of your tale of the 'thirties. I see you walking down some incredibly narrow valley, with the usual assortment of fir trees, steep crags and houses falling into ruin, accompanied by Truth, Beauty and Goodness. Your lady must inevitably be the proud and melancholy child of an ancient and long-decaying family or the miller's beautiful daughter. I await the next chapter – in which you should, by all the rules of the game, interview an old, old servitor and then philosophise a little in the moonlight – with eagerness.

I am writing this in the study. It is late and the owls are hooting from the roof of the big barn. I propose now to dismiss this vaguely melancholy scene by going to bed and reading the memoirs of some sensible eighteenth-century gentleman. And, by the way, have you noticed how fond our bright young intellectuals are becoming of the eighteenth century? What a pity it is, though, that they contrive to overlook its courage and good sense!

Yours,
ROBERT.

STATION HOTEL,
KESWICK.

MY DEAR ROBERT,

Thank you for writing to me just now so frequently. You keep me still in a sane world from which, if it weren't for my touch with you and Marjorie, I should really seem to be excluded. It isn't that this hotel and the people in it aren't sane enough (they most certainly *are*!), but my adventure grows ever weirder and weirder. What you say at the end of your letter about eighteenth-century romances and the rest is, I'm sure, the true prophecy. Odd that you should already know Garrowdale and I not, but to-morrow I penetrate its Radcliffian fastnesses and bang the knocker of Farthing Hall. I feel as though you were with me in this; in fact I have the oddest sense (I seem to be full of these 'senses' just now, although I'm not a bit like the wife of a famous boxer who announced somewhere the other day that 'her hunches were mighty accurate') that you are going later on to be concerned in all of this — and I perhaps in Mrs Masham, Miss Banks and the rest. Who knows? We've never bothered to write to one another so much about people before. I frankly admit that I think it a jolly healthy sign that you should be shaken out of your *Chimera*, though only for a moment, by your Mrs Masham. Events are improving both of us! And, by the way, I like your Miss Banks. Were I not at the moment so completely absorbed in another lady, who knows but that my chivalrous nature——?

But I mustn't poach on your preserves.

Well, after getting my names from Chaplin as I told you in my last letter I spent hours in wondering about my next move. By the way, how long is it since I've spent hours over anything but my painting? Isn't this a holiday? I tell you, Robert, that this preoccupation over someone else, even though I've only seen her for a moment, is new life to me. I'm another creature from the man of a week ago — and what, what am I going to be in six months' time?

What was my next step to be? Should I take the good old convention, drive a car down the valley, break down and beg Farthing Hall for assistance? Should I pretend that I had met Rossett before, or be lost tramping through the hills, or sprain an ankle? First I must know more of the man himself, explain Chaplin's odd comment on him. But here there were difficulties. I didn't want to go poking about the town forcing inquiries. That might make people think, Rossett himself might hear of it. I've developed an amazing carefulness in the last few days, something entirely foreign to my nature, I'm afraid. I thought of approaching Chaplin again – but how odd it would seem to him, this persistent interest of mine in the Rossett family! All the while behind this delicacy of mine there is the thought of Jean, the notion that I might frighten her by acting too quickly or seeming too presumptuous.

Well, there I was, sitting in the bosom of my old friend the hotel's sitting-room, with 'The Hunted Stag' and 'The Duke of Wellington' watching me from the walls, pondering my puzzle, when once again (and this is now the third or fourth time) fate, chance, what you like, stepped in and helped me forward. Sitting opposite to me, close to the very bitter spluttering little fire, was an odd old man. Old? I don't know. Any age. But he was little, with rather long untidy hair, a black cape over his shoulder and his tongue sticking out of his teeth at the excitement of his occupation. And that occupation was sticking stamps into a stamp-album. He had a large dirty envelope filled with stamps, and out of this envelope the stamps were for ever dropping on to the floor, and he saying, 'Tut! Tut!' very vexedly, as he stooped down to pick them up. He was as unaware of me as I am of the Royal Academy, but something drove me – yes, compelled me – to speak to him. I asked him whether Garrowdale was worth a walk. He looked up, dropped a little cloud of stamps, said 'Tut! Tut!' but didn't bend for them, only sat there staring at me. He said Good God, he hadn't a notion there was anyone in the room. When he looked at you he had charming gentle eyes like a friendly unalarmed lamb's, and his voice was soft and acquainted, I'll swear, with the Latin tongue. Sorry, I said, I'd been there ever since breakfast but hadn't wished to disturb him. He smiled then quite delightfully and said it was no disturbance and why did I want to walk up Garrowdale? I said I wasn't sure that I did, but I'd heard that there was a most interesting old house there, Farthing Hall, one of the few really old manor-houses in the district. Liked its name, I said. Romantic situation for a house. Yes, said the old gentleman, very interesting old house, but unfortunately in the possession of a pig. Oh, said I, not fluttering an eyelash, what a pity! Yes, said the old gentleman, quite suddenly indignant, so indignant that he dropped his stamp-book and didn't notice it, not only a Pig but a Ruffian, not only a Ruffian but a Conceited Jackass, not only a Conceited Jackass but a Madman, a Drunkard and a Robber. I said again that it was a shame. Yes, it *was* a shame! His name was Rossett, and it soon appeared that twenty years ago he had had a feud with the old gentleman (who lives, I discovered, now at Cockermouth), because the old gentleman's dog defended himself against a pack of Rossett mongrels. The old gentleman (whose name I at last discovered was Henty) had been taking the merest walk up the valley and with him his dog Buster, and suddenly from nowhere at all the villain Rossett (I have learnt that he is now between sixty and seventy, a huge man apparently with no manners) had appeared with a crowd of dogs who had nearly murdered Buster, but not (this Mr Henty told me with the greatest pride) until Buster had slain one of them. Although it was twenty years ago, to Mr Henty it was as though it had happened yesterday. I was treated to every detail. The quarrel apparently found its way at last into the courts, and Mr Henty was awarded damages, the neighbourhood (according to Mr Henty) hating Rossett and ready to strike at him whenever possible. Now, who would have guessed it? By a miraculous chance I had hit on the one man in the world who was ready to talk about the Rossetts for hours. I won't bore you with all that he told me or even half of it. The main facts are that the Rossetts have lived at Farthing Hall for generations (that Chaplin had already told me), that this man came into the place early, married, killed his wife by violence (so old Henty asserts), married again, killed the second one too, and now for the last ten years has lived there with only his sister and his son and daughter, the son (my young chinless friend) a rotter, made so by his father. Rossett is, according to Henty, hated and feared by all the countryside, but the odd thing is that, as the old gentleman fumed and spluttered, I got an odd picture of this man – against my wishes entirely. Henty admitted that he'd been a handsome devil in his time, that he's courageous as Satan and (most interesting of all these facts to me) that he has apparently a passionate love of his home and the hills and fields around it. Drinks like a fish, has the temper of a madman. Indeed many think he *is* crazy. 'What,' said old Henty, 'that pretty girl does in that household I shudder to think. Nice girl, too.'

'She's pretty?' I asked.

'Very pretty. Quite a child, poor thing. But they say she's devoted to her brother and father.'

That was enough for me. I had all I wanted from the old boy. I walked out to cool my brow. To-morrow I make my attempt, and, upon my soul, Robert, there's an adventure ahead. From somewhere or other I've caught a sense of drama round that man's history. You may say that it's only because he's Jean's father. Not altogether. He must be lonely, poor devil, raging there in that desolate valley, in that old house——. But I won't bore you with my fantasies. Wait for my next letter. You'll get something worth your while!

Yours,

MARK.

PEARTREE LODGE,
LITTLE HURLIFORD,
OXON.

MY DEAR MARK,

One moment. Before you disappear into Farthing Hall, please answer the following questions. Am I – in your opinion – selfish? Am I an intellectual snob? Am I a prig? Am I an egoist? Have I ever reminded you of Malvolio, Sir Charles Grandison, the unrepentant Darcy, young Pendennis, Sir Willoughby Patterne? This is not an extension of one of those insufferably personal games that some people like to play after dinner. Nor is it – worse luck – a joke. I have just been accused of selfishness, intellectual snobbery, priggishness, and egoism, and by a person who considers that she knows me better than anybody else in the world and who has certainly had her opportunities of forming a judgment. Yes, Marjorie has just been accusing me of all these things.

She really did make accusations. It wasn't merely a matter of calling names. If it had been, I should not feel so troubled. Marjorie is one of those people (and you are another of them) who are so quick-tempered that when they quarrel they use words as if they were brickbats, hurling the first that come to hand. Thus if Marjorie were to have a row with some very ascetic Church dignitary (and it would not take her long), she would be just as likely to call him a drunkard and a glutton as anything else. As soon as the row is over, she rushes forward to explain that she didn't mean anything she said. 'I was so furious,' she will confess, 'and of course I had to say *something*.' And I defy any man to remain angry in the face of such a confession. But this time it was not mere name-calling but something cooler and harder. Very quietly, quite calmly, she has just accused me of being all the things I have mentioned. Perhaps you can hardly say she accused me, for even that suggests a certain degree of warmth. She simply pointed out these things.

She came in here about an hour ago, picked up a book and put it down again, and then said, quite casually: 'I've got a new secretary for Mrs Masham. It's Adela Bilthorpe. She was at school with me. You met her once in town, do you remember? She's just wired to say she'll take the job and come down here to-morrow morning.'

I said that it seemed a pity because Adela Bilthorpe appeared to be a sensible girl.

'I know she's very hard up,' Marjorie went on, very quietly. 'She says she's delighted. And I know that she's met Mrs Masham several times.'

'I'm sorry she's so very hard up as all that,' I murmured.

Marjorie gave me one of those wide cool stares that suggest to you that you are back again in knickerbockers, screaming on the nursery floor. A few years ago I should have felt guilty, a naughty small boy, but now the trick no longer works. I faced that stare and remained an adult male of forty years with no more illusions than are necessary in order to remain comfortable. Indeed I smiled and began to fill a pipe.

'Adela Bilthorpe arrives to-morrow morning,' she said, after a pause. 'Then she and Mrs Masham leave after lunch, on the two-fifteen train.'

'It's incredible!' I grinned at her. 'I knew that two-fifteen would come into its own at last.'

Marjorie gave one of her little shrugs and walked over to the window. 'You realise, of course,' she began, without turning round, 'that you've been appallingly rude to Mrs Masham, and that she's noticed it and been hurt, very hurt. She'd have gone long ago if I had not pressed her to stay and apologised for your rudeness.'

'That was exceedingly kind of you, my dear.' I was rather annoyed at this. 'But wasn't it rather absurd keeping her here to be apologised to? Haven't you only yourself to blame?'

'I told her that you didn't mean to be rude, had no intention of snubbing her. I had to paint a picture of you as the dreamy recluse, the eccentric and absent-minded scholar. Then she didn't mind. She happens to have a great admiration for you, in her own queer muddled fashion.'

'Then all's well,' I put in, perhaps too complacently.

'No, it isn't.' She turned round now and looked at me. 'You see, Robert, even if she didn't care, I did. You ask me why I pressed her to stay. The very question gives you away. Because you didn't want her here, then she had to go at once or be insulted. You forget there are two people living in this house. It never occurs to you that *my* life, not a bit of it but the whole of it, is passed here, that I've absolutely nothing else. To you it's only a kind of — what do they call it? — oh, yes — a base of operations, but to me it's almost everything. And that's why I asked Hilda Masham to stay. I wanted to give you a hint that I was here too, a real person and not a shadow of yourself——'

'This is absurd, Marjorie,' I interrupted. I wanted to say a thousand things at once, her attitude was so preposterous, but before I could begin she was off again.

'I was afraid you would say that,' she remarked, very calmly. 'I'm not going to say much more. It's useless talking. You see, Robert, it's rapidly becoming impossible for me to live with you and keep my self-respect. Yes, it's as bad as that. You're turning yourself into the kind of husband that any sensible woman, who doesn't believe in the martyrdom or self-mortification idea of marriage, dreads most of all – the very worst kind.'

'What!' I'm afraid I shouted, but I could hardly believe my ears. She was so quiet too.

She laughed, shortly and not very pleasantly. 'Oh, of course you don't come home drunk or beat me or make love to other women. As a matter of fact, you couldn't fall in love now, Robert; your pride wouldn't let you. But these may not be the things that a woman resents most. She might put up with them so long as she remained a real person to the man and was fond of him. You don't do any of these terrible things. You're kind, frightfully kind, but you've contrived to forget that I'm a real person. I've watched you forgetting. For you there is only one life here now, and that is your own.'

'Nonsense, Marjorie,' I told her. 'It's no use. You can't fit me into the part of domestic tyrant; it's ludicrous. And as the crushed and misunderstood wife, you're not a bit convincing. We're not beginning a new three-act comedy——'

'Can't you see?' she cried, impatiently. Then she quietened down again, spoke quite softly. 'I'm going to speak plainly, Robert. I've been thinking a lot about it lately – oh, not these last few days, but for months and months now. This is only the climax.'

I told her that at any rate I was glad we had now reached the climax. That was something.

She brushed this aside, and went on: 'It's really like a bad fairy tale. You've become exactly the kind of man you used to detest so much – pointing them out whenever we met them – in the old days. It's queer, but it's true, horribly true. I should laugh if it weren't you. You once gave me a definition of a bad husband – do you remember – and now——' She broke off and stared at the opposite wall.

'I used to talk a good deal about bad husbands,' I said rather grimly. 'And a good deal about marriage in general, knowing nothing about it. The only thing I know about marriage now is that it never ceases to be surprising, though not always pleasantly surprising. You might be good enough to explain what rotten bad kind of husband I happen to be. I never flattered myself that I was exemplary, but still——'

'Oh, how heavy and pompous you are!' she cried. 'Well, you want to know, so I will tell you. You're selfish. You're an intellectual snob. You're a prig. And you're an egoist, yes, an egoist. And any woman who lived with you a week would tell you so. No, I've finished.' She turned away and ran out of the room.

I don't know what to say. I don't think I want to say anything. You notice that I began this letter lightly enough, asking you if you too see me in this strange light. But that was some time ago, for I've smoked several pipes at odd intervals during the telling of this domestic tale, this idyll of the Cotswolds. I know what you will say – that everything must be set right at once. But, you see, if I am the kind of man Marjorie says I am, then it's no use my making even a beginning to set things right. And if I am not that kind of man, then it's equally useless my trying to talk it out with a woman who can misjudge me so grossly. This sounds reasonable, though I am not sure that it really is, and I am too tired to care.

Go to Garrowdale, girl or no girl. I wish I was exploring it with you, though at the moment I think we make better correspondents than we should companions. Your nonsense would hardly suit my nonsense; but we do well enough on paper.

Your ancient friend,
ROBERT.

STATION HOTEL,
KESWICK.

MY DEAR BOB,

What a bewildering accumulation of events! Here am I packing up, about to move on into the very heart of my adventure, burning to sit down and tell you all about it, when your last letter arrives, making me feel how selfish I am to trouble you with my small affairs. Your letter indeed has made me feel very uncomfortable. Reading between the lines I know that you are acutely unhappy. Although I'm in years so much younger there has always been unspoken between us (may I say it without sentimentality?) a very especial bond of trust and understanding that we have neither of us quite had with anyone else.

Friendship, of course, is different from love and marriage — it occupies another kind of territory and one of the conditions of its atmosphere is a sort of brusque pretence of indifference. We've joked and argued and growled and grumbled together so naturally that we've seemed often to take our relationship entirely for granted — but for myself I can only say that it is one of the finest things I've ever got out of life or ever will get, and for trust and confidence is not to be beaten. I say all this because I feel that you're very lonely. It is the very moment of all the years of our friendship that I oughtn't to have left you. For God's sake, old man, don't let a ridiculous old woman make serious trouble between yourself and Marjorie. I'm truly alarmed by your last letter. I don't like the undertone of it.

As soon as I've settled into my new quarters — which will be this evening — address The Brown Bull, Garrowdale — I'll sit down and write you a letter all about yourself and Marjorie. Just what I think of you both. Things I've never told you before! You look out!

Well, I've invaded the ogre in his castle. The plot develops wonderfully. You just listen.

Yesterday afternoon I started out in a car hired from Mr Pape, a thick-set, contemptuous old boy with brindled hair driving me. It was just the right kind of day for my adventure — misty, low-hanging breaking clouds, the colour of the hills just turning, patches of purple, amber, brown scattered about as though someone were trying to decide which colour would really suit this particular autumn mist. Thick bulging clouds like smoke, with drifts of blue sky, but everything low in tone, faint and

veiled. We started through Keswick and out to Portinscale. I soon saw
that my companion was deeply curious as to what I wanted to go to
Garrowdale for, but his Cumberland reticence held him reluctantly back.
No one, I soon learnt, ever went up Garrowdale except the inhabitants of
that lonely valley. You see it was the gate to nowhere. There was a kind
of rough way over into Wastdale, but so wet and dreary that no one save
shepherds bothered with it. In the winter it must be a desolate place to
live. He wouldn't spend his time there not if you gave him a fortune. Not
a decent house of any size there except Farthing Hall, and that was a
queer place enough. What was queer, I asked him? Oh, he didn't know.
Folk's tales mostly. They said there was a ghost, a long tall man in a night-
shirt. He didn't believe in ghosts himself. But Mr Rossett who lived there
was a funny-tempered gentleman. Fine figure of a man or had been once.
Some say he's queer in the head.

I asked him no more questions. I didn't, for some odd reason, want any
answers. I had a strange sense that I must make up my mind for myself; it
was *my* adventure, in which no one else was concerned.

We had, by this time, started up the valley. A queer, indeterminate little
road that seemed as though it were never going to make up its mind
whether it were worth while going on, an odd mumbling stream hidden
often by deep bramble and dark trees, nothing overhead but the clouds that
seemed ever to hang lower and lower, a little chill in the air not unpleasant,
and all the colours of sky and hill and road and stream misted and dim.

For a long time we never exchanged a word. Then he suddenly asked
me what was my destination.

'I'd like to have a look at Farthing Hall,' I said.

And at that spoken word I had the queerest conviction that every stock
and stone, blade and branch answered me: 'Oh, you shall! You jolly well
shall! You shall see Farthing Hall all right!'

The chauffeur didn't answer me. They are laconic, these fellows. Not
for them to reason why. There was one cloud like a fat man with a
gigantic toothache that hung over the valley's end, almost exactly
balanced on the high tip of a purple hill. If you pricked it with a lance it
would burst and flood the valley with dirty water. That's how it seemed
to me.

We passed scarcely a house and never a human, and then, quite
suddenly, just as things happen in a dream, all the hills closed in about us,
as though they'd suddenly stepped forward under secret command to see
that we didn't escape, and then, just after my awareness of this, there on
the right, back from the road on rising ground, was Farthing Hall.

I can't give you now half the description of it that I hope to give you
later. I have, looking back this morning, a strangely indistinct vision of it.
I know that there was a thick hedge with some untidy figures, a peacock

and so on, cut on top; there was a rough path running up from the gate through a neglected garden that had in its centre a sundial and a ragged square of flags. The house itself seemed to me a cross between modern farm and eighteenth-century manor, but this I won't swear to. It had many windows, some of them blocked in, crooked chimneys, and an air of standing crossly, rather viciously and *very* obstinately full square to all the winds. It was naked but contemptuous. Behind it, without hedge or wall, was the moor running up to three crumpled inquisitive hills that seemed to be leaning forward to pick up anything they might overhear.

As we came up to it I saw that the gate was open, and then, amazingly, the front door, and standing in it as though he were there expecting me a huge clumsy man in rather shabby tweeds, no hat on his head, three dogs at his feet, and (as I remember now, looking back), a strangely intriguing dark hall with white stone flags and a black staircase behind him.

Our car stopped, and the dogs rushed down the garden yelling like the fiend. He waited a moment, and then, as the car stayed there, came leisurely with a heavy, rather swinging, movement to the gate. He kicked one of the dogs that was near him and cursed the others. Then he stood at the gate waiting. For a moment there was a curious silence, while we looked at one another. In that instant he stamped himself on my memory for ever – a man between sixty and seventy, a rather curious round close-cropped, bullet-shaped head, black thick eyebrows, face round, flushed with little purple lines, a short-clipped grey moustache – not a *bad* face, but I could see the temper and dissipation clear enough – and a positively huge form, or it seemed so in that dim half light, broad, thick, and, I should guess, a good six foot four in height.

It was plainly for me to speak, so I said:

'Can you tell me whether there's any place near here where I can put up for the night?'

He answered curtly:

'There's the Brown Bull half a mile back.'

'Thanks,' I answered. 'Is it clean?'

'Clean enough,' he replied.

'I'm so sorry to have bothered you,' I said.

'Oh, that's all right.' He looked at me intently for a moment and I at him. I had a consciousness, right or wrong I don't know, that he badly needed company; lonely he seemed with not a soul about, not a sound in the air, the three hills watching, the toothache cloud malevolently motionless.

'Good day,' I said.

'Good day,' he answered, still looking at me. He was, I think, on the edge of saying something further. But he didn't. He turned back up the path, the dogs following him.

And that's all for the present. Jean's father, Jean's house, Jean's lover close to her although she doesn't know it. And now you realise why your letters – continue to write often and fully – must go, until further notice, to the Brown Bull, Garrowdale. I go there early this afternoon.

Your friend,
MARK.

PEARTREE LODGE,
LITTLE HURLIFORD,
OXON.

MY DEAR MARK,

I remember your Brown Bull. I was there sixteen years ago, when I walked over from Borrowdale with Slingsby, an Oxford contemporary of mine who is now Professor of Philosophy at some American university. It was late when we arrived at the Brown Bull, and we were very tired and very hungry. They set before us a gigantic dish of ham and eggs — enough, you would have thought, for six people — and we ate the lot, or at least Slingsby did. He was a huge fellow, with a mop of curly hair and a shining prow of a nose, who had a passion for eating, drinking, smoking, walking and metaphysical argument. He was a thoroughgoing idealist (I mean in metaphysics) and always denied that matter had any reality, though he carried about sixteen and a half stone of it round himself. We had been arguing all day, and the Brown Bull found us still arguing. I can see and hear Slingsby now: his vast face aglow, walking into the ham and eggs, swigging pint after pint of beer, and crying 'But, Newlands, you sceptical rat, can't you see that this table is only an idea! You and I invented it. If we didn't, explain the secondary qualities.' And in order to add emphasis to his statement that the table wasn't really there, he would bang it with his pint mug, and this brought the landlady into the room. Then Slingsby would come out of his metaphysical dream to stare at her and then say: 'Oh, yes! Of course! Could we have some more beer?' I must write to Slingsby to remind him of those daft happy days and to ask him how he fares among the snow and hot dust, the cereals and ice cream, the synthetic gin and the jazz, the luncheon clubs and solemn conventions, of his distant prairie. They must think him a very queer fish out there, though I will wager that his students (if he has any) adore him. But I do not imagine that you want to know anything more about Slingsby, even though you sit in the very room where once he quaffed and roared.

Indeed, although your friendly concern in the last letter warms my heart, I do not imagine that you find it easy to think about Little Hurliford at all. It is obvious that the present adventure (it's your own word) has you in thrall. I would never have thought it possible to receive from you several letters in which there was not a whisper of tones and

planes and values, of canvas and palette and sketch-book. Is this Mark
French, hitherto nothing but an eye and a hand? This fellow who
penetrates into Garrowdale – perhaps the best of all those dales, and one
that has never been touched – and does not even mention his sketch-
book, never seems to be lifting a hand to a pencil – can this be Mark
French, most ambitious, most grimly industrious, of young painters, who
came to the wise conclusion a year or two ago that he could best hope to
achieve something great in art not by talking bad aesthetics in cafés and
philandering at studio parties but by feasting his eyes whenever he could
and then painting and drawing and drawing and painting until he had
squeezed out the last little flicker of light? (That sentence is so long that I
nearly lost you in the middle of it.) It's possible, of course, that you are
going on as usual but that in your letters you are simply concentrating on
the adventure, the *unpainting* and *unsketching* part. If so, I shall feel
relieved. Do have a go at the country – if the image of Miss Jean Rossett
isn't troubling you too much. Nobody except C.J. Holmes has got near
those hills yet. I know half a dozen artists, good men too, who have gone
up there, stared, sighed, and returned empty-handed and head-shaking. If
Miss Rossett is foolish enough not to want to improve her acquaintance
with a very promising young artist, sound in wind and limb, neither
pimply nor squeaking, bright of eye and steady of hand (it sounds like a
ballad), who grows ecstatic at the mere thought of her existence, then
you can fly back to pencil and paper and probably forget her in trying to
capture the lines of those Garrowdale hills. That is where the artist scores.

I envy you that. The writer has to have his mind at ease, unless, of
course, he happens to be writing on the very thing that is troubling him.
He's compelled to spin the stuff out of himself, and if something agitates
him, if he takes to brooding, he cannot even make a beginning. At this
present moment I ought to be considering, most scrupulously, the ideas,
the dreams and idiocies, of the old German Romantics, but my mind
refuses to entertain any thoughts of them. These last few days, they all
become faded little figures, manikins made of ink and dusty paper. I
cannot attend to their dream dramas when I find myself in the middle of
a real live comedy, wondering what will happen to me in the next act.
The nearest I can get to my *Chimera of Romanticism* just now is the
reading of your letters.

But if I were an artist, I could still go and draw something. Some little
crisis in your personal life will close your mind to anything else, but it
won't shut your eyes, which are still open to their impressions of form
and colour. And your hand is still waiting there, ready to curve round. If
you were in my place, you would probably be working like blazes, not
producing any masterpieces, I imagine, but still quite happily occupied.
Moreover, an artist is able to do – quite conscientiously – such a lot of

cheerful pottering about. The curse of writing is that there's no pottering about: either you are at work or you are not. I can't amuse myself putting out fifteen different kinds of paper, mixing little pots of coloured inks, and so on and so forth: there are no opportunities for that sort of thing, which is all very pleasant, healthy, heart-easing. Half the work of an artist seems to me to be like being a boy again, left alone with a new large box of tools. You are lucky fellows. Spare a moment to pity your stooping, dusty, blear-eyed brethren of the quill, who cannot relieve their feelings in great glorious daubs of crimson lake.

Just now we are being treated to the very best early autumn weather, mornings of smoke and level gold light, evenings of slate-grey and scarlet fantasies in the sky: you know what I mean. I am in the mood, though, when one doesn't attend to these things, when Nature seems to be something going on at the other side of a colossal plate-glass window, that of a shop at which one never thinks of buying anything. Nevertheless, I spent the whole of yesterday out walking, and so missed the arrival and departure of Adela Bilthorpe (*vice* Banks) and the final exit of the Masham. To-day this has been a very silent house. I am keeping my selfish, priggish, egoistical self away from Marjorie, with whom I have not exchanged a word for about thirty-six hours, indeed, only seen twice, I think. You can make what you please of this: say I'm sulking, say I'm hurt, say what you like. To-morrow I go walking again, though this country here is too soft and docile for ten-hour tramps. You feel as if you were bullying it.

Yours,
ROBERT.

THE BROWN BULL,
GARROWDALE.

MY DEAR BOB,

It is four days now since I last wrote to you. It isn't because I haven't wanted to. This new habit of mine of putting everything on to paper and then sending it to you does no harm, and gives me a lot of pleasure.

I like to make you see all this as vividly as I can partly because I feel that you share it with me and partly because I must have someone to pour it out to. That's the necessity for a lover, I find – a confidant. I'd heard it and read it often enough, but it never struck me that it could be true. Everything else that I have felt deeply in life I've buried down in myself – when my father died, the afternoon I finished the painting of my 'Silver Interior' (that was the first time that I was *sure* I was a painter), my first trip through Spain, the two days in the Prado, these, and other things, I've always kept to myself. You've complained sometimes that I never tell you the *real* things. But now I can't tell you enough – I want you to share in everything. Oh Robert, if only you'd seen her – only once – just a glimpse of her, I think you'd understand. Or would you? It is a never-ending surprise with what differences people see other people, and with what differences one sees other people oneself when the mood, the whim, the passion is over. Nearly always – but *not* every time – I should never change in my affection for you now, no, not whatever you did. Or at least so I think. But suppose it was something very bad, something mean and cruel? But then you couldn't, you being you. That's the answer. But couldn't you? How does one know? When I think of the things that I could do, the beastly rotten crawly things. Or am I just trying to make myself interesting to myself?

Yes, enough of this. It isn't really my job, as you say in your last letter. Oh, wait a minute, I've something to say about that letter. But first let me tell you where I am and how I feel here. I came out here four days ago with my very limited luggage and a parcel of books snatched from Chaplin, mostly little cheap editions. Would you like to know what they are? Reynolds's *Discourses*, *Arabia Deserta* (the truncated one-volume edition), *Return of the Native* (Is Hardy as good a novelist as it's the fashion of you literary dogs to declare? I'm not at all sure), Houghton's *Keats* (just out in the little Everyman), *Don Quixote*, two Phillips Oppenheims (he's so much better than his companions, Wallace and the others), *The*

Highways and Byways: Lake District, Humphry Clinker and *Eothen.* That's the lot. It's a nice little pub. Very simple. Downstairs, bar, room for meals, rough little smoking-room; upstairs, narrow creaky passage, several bedrooms and the usual offices. My room is pleasant save for the wall-paper which tells in yellow tones of a battle apparently between wasps and beetles with an occasional sunflower thrown in for luck. That's the best that I can make of it. There's a text and a looking-glass, a bed, a small table, two chairs. From the window there's a view — a lane with geese, a fragment of the valley river, a few sloping fields and the three crinkly hills behind Farthing Hall. I can't actually see Farthing Hall, but I know just where it is. I'm in touch with it. She's only half a mile away. Is it a wonder that I feel as though I were at the gates of Paradise?

If I could tear down the wall-paper, distemper the walls and hang up a Manet, I could be happy here for donkey's years. Which Manet would I choose? 'Le Linge' with its ridiculous behatted child, or the adorable Luxembourg 'Le Balcon,' the enchanting angel with the parasol, the dark woman with the tragic unhappy face, or 'Le Bon Bock' just to cheer me up and prevent my feeling lonely, or the divine 'Déjeuner sur l'Herbe' that there was all the row about, so that I should always have sunshine and happiness and perfect freedom here in the room with me. Have you ever noticed the flowers lying among the clothes in the left-hand corner of that picture? Miraculously painted wonders! Now I think of it I would be willing to have just that left-hand corner of the 'Déjeuner,' frame it, and put it on this wall. How would that fragment of colour get on with the text on the opposite wall? It's a good text too. 'The Lord is my shepherd. . . . He leadeth me beside the still waters.' They'd settle down all right.

I'm writing to the light of a shuddering despairing candle. And it's late. I must stop. I've said nothing about your last letter though. I feel in it that you're writing to cover your emotion. You hate this row with Marjorie, don't you? The first bad one, so far as I know, that you've ever had. I feel as though it were bad somehow. I'll make you angry perhaps by saying that I think there's truth in some of her accusations. I've been waiting for something of this kind. Writing seems to make a man selfish in a way that painting doesn't — or rather it produces another kind of selfishness. Perhaps that's what you mean when you say that you envy the painter. I don't know what the difference is, but of almost all the male writers I know I think it can truthfully be said that their wives are too dominating or too submissive. They haven't struck the right compromise somehow. And I know so many painters who are happily married — Colles, Shorncliffe, Mason, Edges, Foster — lots more. But of course you *are* happily married. You love Marjorie, and Marjorie most certainly loves you — but you've taken it all too much for granted. She's been so sweet to you for so long that you don't consider it a miracle any longer. You did at first. You wondered how she could care for such an old bear, such an unattractive, ugly – all the rest of it. I remember all the things you said. Now you think it quite natural that she should. You've gone up a bit in your own estimation, and she's gone down a little – just because she's been so good to you. Oh, I know it's easy for outsiders to talk, but there *is* something in it. You're not a conceited man, far from it – but you are conceited about your ideas. You get a good idea and before you've had time to find out that you aren't up to the idea – when you become much more modest than you've any right to be – you're simply on the top of the world. That's when you're hard to bear and think Marjorie a lucky woman to have you for a companion. Painters deal very little in ideas – or they oughtn't to – and the thing they're after is from the beginning so far beyond and above them that they haven't time for much self-elation. Not that there aren't conceited painters, I know plenty, but they're small fry. But was Gauguin conceited, or Van Gogh, or Manet, or Corot, or Courbet, or Rembrandt, or Velazquez? Arrogant, impatient, untidy, impossible, but conceited never.

Yes, I must go to bed. The candle's in its last gutter, and the shadows leaping on the wall are drunken like intoxicated rabbits. Four days I've been here. Not a glimpse of her and not courage enough to break into the house. Through all this adventure my conduct's been a queer mixture of courage and diffidence – one following the other – so to-morrow I'm due for an adventure. The candle at its last leap tells me there'll be one. Good night, old Robert. Remember I'll come if you send for me. Yes, even though I'm at the very moment climbing the Farthing Hall staircase.

Affectionately,

MARK.

THE BROWN BULL,
GARROWDALE.

MY DEAR BOB,

Now I've got something to write to you about. This will be a long
screed. I'm quite unable to sleep. I've just come back to this quiet little
tallow-smelling room after one of the most disturbing evenings of my life.
I've got an extra candle here, one of twelve fat proud virgin ones, that
will last me all night if I want it to. You shall have all the adventure, every
bit of it. I don't know whether I'm happy or sad, triumphant or
despairing. But first the preliminaries.

Yesterday – the day after I wrote to you last – was lovely weather, with
a round red sun and a pale glassy blue sky. So I took sandwiches and
Houghton's *Keats* and walked. Where, I can't exactly tell you, except that
by the middle of the day I was on the moor with a blue baby-faced tarn
just behind me and below me half of Buttermere Lake and the valley. I
went out to clear my head, and clear my head I did. It was cold and a
little frosty, very bright and still. I read Keats's letters, the early ones
before he was unhappy, and thought what a fool I'd been to let these days
pass by without any action. I got a kind of assurance from somewhere
that she was wanting me, waiting for me, wondering why I didn't come.

Early in the afternoon I started down again and at last just as dusk was
gathering I turned into the road only a mile or so from the Brown Bull.
There was a lovely faint purple light, a tang of blackberries and silver in
the air if you get a painter's sense of it. The long walk and fine air had
done me a world of good. My head was up. I was thinking of a mix of
things, Keats and Fanny Brawne and Constable's 'Hay Cart' and some
street in London with a curiosity shop whose windows are always filled
with green and purple glass bottles, and Steak Minute and Cheese
Soufflé, and that end of Buttermere where the little sandy beach runs, all
things and anything and nothing, when – I ran straight into a heather-
smelling waistcoat, a bunch of hard buttons and, as I clutched it to keep
myself from falling, flesh (rather a lot of it) and bones under the
waistcoat. Someone cursed and swore, dogs barked, I apologised and – it
was Rossett of Farthing Hall.

He was angry and, I think, funnily enough, frightened. I suppose that
he has a lot of enemies round here. Years of looking out for them have
spoiled his nerves. Then he recognised me and was suddenly pleased.

'And how's the Brown Bull?' he asked me. Even as he spoke to me he jerked his head about in an odd way as though he couldn't be sure that there wasn't still someone hanging about in the hedge waiting to give him a knock.

I told him the Brown Bull was all right, and he said he was glad to hear it. Then we started walking up the road, the dogs quietly at his heels, the place silent altogether save for the running stream. The purple faded out of the sky and the stars came out one after the other. He lifted up his head and sniffed; 'Good air,' he said. Then, very abruptly: 'I love this place. I hope you do.' I said, indeed I did. He asked me whether I were on holiday. I answered that I was a painter, that I'd never been up to this part before, and that it was more beautiful than I had supposed. He said that he'd lived here all his life, that he couldn't breathe anywhere else. We had reached the Brown Bull. We stopped abruptly. He asked me whether I were alone. 'Quite,' I answered.

'You may as well come in and have some supper with us to-morrow evening,' he said. 'Dull for you sitting alone there in that pub.'

I thanked him and accepted. He told me the hour and that I wasn't to dress, and strode off. So it had come! At last it had come! I was to sit at her table, break bread with her. And what would she say to this, how would she behave? Would she be angry, would she tell her father that we'd met before, would she be cold and distant?

I didn't care. I felt that I was up to any situation. *And* I was happy. I went to bed that night like a king.

And now to my amazement I'm terribly sleepy. I can't keep my eyes open. To-night's adventure has tired me more than I knew. I'll go on to-morrow. Good night, Bob. I can hardly write my name. I print it in capital letters,

MARK.

Later.

Do you know it's the oddest thing — I've slept without stirring, without dreaming, until ten o'clock of the morning. I don't believe I've ever in my life done that before. I seem to have crossed over some dividing line in my life last night. That moment under the candles when the grandfather clock suddenly shuddered and, looking up, I caught her gaze . . . it's all dark and fantastic to me this morning, the colours of that house. I don't believe any of it's real — not the Rossetts, nor that house, nor the absurd parrot, nor that temper and agitation . . . but I'll give you the events in order.

At the proper time I walked along the road to the house. It was the loveliest evening, quiet as the sky in Lorenzo di Credi's 'Nativity.' Such silence I think I've never known before. My heels on the road made an uncanny sound. I tell you about all this quiet because of what happened afterwards. Until I put my hand on the latch of that gate I was in a world of frozen stillness. Once through the gate and the barking of the dogs broke everything into fragments. I didn't see the brutes; they were all shut up, but they put my back up as barking dogs do when you come to a house. You've been walking along, rather pleased with yourself, perhaps, and thinking the people you're visiting are rather lucky to have you as a guest, when the damned dogs make you feel a stranger and a fool. The front door opened and Rossett came out to meet me. There were lamps burning in the hall behind him; he was wearing a dark-coloured jacket and some kind of loose wide trousers, and a fine figure of a man he looked standing there. As I came up he sniffed the air again as though he couldn't have enough of it and he held out his hands, the palms upward, as though to feel the breath of the wind on them. I liked him, to tell you the truth, better just then than I was going to for the rest of the evening. There was the hall with its white-flagged floor and old dark staircase, and opening out of it a sitting-room with windows looking to the hills. The door between the hall and the sitting-room was open. There was a lamp in the hall and another in the room beyond, but they gave very insufficient light and I can't possibly make you feel the real discomfort that I felt or give you adequate reasons for it. There was something perhaps in the rather stale, musty smell that there was, and then oddly with that there seemed to be a lot of breeze, curtains blowing, something creaking, a distant door banging, but in spite of that no air.

The sitting-room — all in half shadow — into which we went was filled with old-fashioned things. You could hardly move because of them — old photographs, old albums with heavy shining covers, old china and little old boxes. The carpet and the wall-paper were faded, and in that dim light looked like green water. The carpet was thin under one's foot. There was a stone floor that struck chill through the carpet. A small hissing fire in the grate. Oh, I don't know, Robert, I can't describe these things. It's a painter's description, and yet seems to leave out all the essentials. We were alone there anyway, and we went and stood by the window. A most uncomfortable five minutes followed, and neither of us said a word. We were standing quite close to one another — his shoulder touched mine. I'm afraid I felt a sort of physical fear of him. He seemed so large and thick and strong. It was as though with one hand he could strangle me, pick me up, quietly open the window and throw me out on to the moor. I felt that now that he'd got me there he was simply bored to tears. I felt his violence just beating through the room.

Anyway we neither of us said a word. I'm not at a loss as a rule, but I could think of nothing whatever to say. At last to my intense relief a tall thin woman with the face of a hungry sheep came in, and, just behind her, Jean. That fearful overwhelming agitation again. The room swam, the hungry sheep ran into the fire, Rossett flew to the ceiling. But I beat it down; I knew that I must show nothing, that if ever in my life I must be calm it was then. She was dressed in a very simple black dress. I was introduced first to the sheep, Miss Rossett, Rossett's sister. She bleated and then the moment came. Jean had not, of course, dreamt that it would be me. When she recognised me her hand trembled for an instant against mine. She gave no other sign. She moved away, back into the shadow.

Then the chinless brother came in, and I realised instantly another thing. He hated me on sight. He didn't recognise me, of course. He hadn't even seen me in Keswick, and at the theatre for only a moment. But he felt something. Who knows what these intuitions are? I can only repeat, he hated me on sight. Very soon afterwards we moved into a very dark little dining-room and sat down to a chilly meal. I say chilly with justice, because although a fire was burning there was this same damp musty air here that I had noticed in the other rooms.

The food was bad, and only one person spoke – that person was our host. I have been wrong perhaps in giving him until now a sinister air, because his megalomania was comic. He had secured in me what I suppose he had been wanting for months, an audience, and out it all came – his ancestors, his parents and at last himself. His birth, suckling, first primer, first orchard-robbing and so on – and then, out of this, his courage, his wisdom, his grand generosities, his inventiveness, his genius, and then out of these again the injustice of the general world, the prejudices of the Deity, and from *these* the scoundrelcies, villainies, falsities, abominations of the immediate neighbourhood, or rather of the whole district from Keswick to Seascale, from Kendal to Cockermouth.

Now he was at last in his favourite country, and indeed he let himself go. The table and everything on it shook with his denunciations, the veins in his neck swelled and a wild frenzied look came into his eyes. The madness of the megalomaniac!

No one else said anything. The Sheep made winks and mutterings at the clumsy little north-country servant. Brother Oaf sat there swilling his food and every once and again giving me an offensive stare. Jean was acutely miserable. I dared to hope that it was because she did not wish to show me this intimate picture of her family life, and I tried to catch her gaze, but always she avoided it.

Until the end of the meal. Then just as we were about to rise the grandfather clock in the hall gave a crazy wheeze, a parrot in a gilt cage near the window screeched out 'Polly! Polly! Polly!' in a voice of shrieking rage and some of the coal in the grate crashed together. It was, I suppose, the sudden simultaneousness of these noises, but Rossett half jumped to his feet, gripped the table with his thick purple-veined hands, and shouted, turning to the bird, 'Curse you! Damn your bloody noise!' It was at that moment that I caught Jean's gaze. Of what did I not try to reassure her in that moment – of escape and freedom and happiness, anything in the world that I could give her. I don't know now whether she was regarding me with friendliness or annoyance. At least I can be certain of the brother. He had caught my glance.

'And what sort of rot do you paint?' he asked me as we rose from our chairs. He had been drinking a lot of whisky, as indeed was his usual habit, I've no doubt. I answered him casually as we went into the other room. My thoughts were too full of Jean to bother about him.

The old man was full of amiability again. He took my arm and led me about showing me things. I daresay you, if you were to see him, would find him a kind of jolly Falstaffian fellow, much more farcical than anything else – you have that gift – but I just hated him as we moved about, his hand gripping my arm. I loathed that he should touch me. And then he said something that made my heart stop beating. He pointed to a photograph of a stout rough-looking farmer sort of fellow.

'My daughter's fiancé,' he said. 'Gentleman farmer quite near here. They'll be married in a month or two. Good chap. Only man I like round here.'

So that was it, was it? I felt a kind of sick disappointment and then a rough resolved obstinacy. I was certain that, following the good old novel tradition, this was a marriage into which she was being driven. But in any case this meant that I had not much time to lose. By good fortune a moment later I had a chance of a word alone with her. Rossett and his son were called by something into the hall.

'Please forgive me,' I said, 'this further coincidence.'

'What have you come here for?' she asked me quickly.

'To see the valley,' I answered.

'You swear that's all?'

'There'll be another reason,' I went on quickly, eagerly, 'if you'll think of me as a friend. If I can help——'

'I don't know you,' she said, looking nervously into the hall.

'You can,' I said, 'if you want to.'

'Then,' she went on swiftly, 'please don't come here. There's nothing for anyone in this house. We never have visitors. Don't come – *please* don't come.'

'Tell me one thing,' I went on urgently. 'Is it true that you're going to be married soon?'

She nodded her head.

'And to that man?' I pointed to the photograph.

'Yes,' she said.

'You don't love him. You can't. Why are you marrying him?'

She hadn't time to answer. The men came back.

I left half an hour later. Chiefly because the young man (his Christian name was Walter) was so insufferably rude. His every word was a sneer. He wanted, I could see, to provoke me to a quarrel. The older Rossett, on the other hand, wished to be friendly, and at last when I was going walked with me to the gate, his hand on my arm, pressing me to come again. I walked back to the inn in a state of great despondency. I didn't see — I don't see — what my next step is to be. The girl is to be married in a few months' time. She doesn't care a farthing for me. Why should she? I love her more deeply every time that I set eyes on her. And it is that, Bob, that sends me on. Loving her as I do I have no choice. I must help her and soon. I can only enter the house through the father's good will, so the father's good will I must have. And the father is a crazy megalomaniac bore. Poor Jean! Her mother must have been a nice woman and must have suffered too. Anyway I must get her out of this. Your advice will be welcome. I feel at the moment helpless. I'm not, you see, accustomed to these melodramatic situations. It's really not my line.

                                                                        Yours ever,
                                                                        MARK.

PEARTREE LODGE,
LITTLE HURLIFORD,
OXON.

MY DEAR MARK,

Marjorie has gone. She went this afternoon, or at least I imagine so. I think I told you that I intended to pass this day walking over the neighbouring Downs. On my way back, at Hatcham, I ran into Blair, who insisted on my having dinner with them. So I stayed and then returned by train. It's queer, but as soon as I set foot in the house I had a feeling that something was wrong. It's true that the maids had gone to bed, but then they usually do go about half-past nine or so. And Marjorie might easily have been over at the Curtis's or have turned in early herself. But no, I felt at once that this was different. I have known the house as quiet but never so *expectantly* quiet. It was just as if the hall were on tiptoe and holding its breath. There were two letters on the hall-table. One was a letter from you. The other was a sealed note from Marjorie. It told me, very briefly, that she had decided to leave me, for reasons she need not specify, and that we could make our arrangements later. She was leaving so hastily because she suddenly felt she could not remain in the house a moment longer, but I should be making a grave mistake if I imagined she was acting on impulse, gratifying a sudden whim. She had thought it all out, as I ought to have seen for myself when she spoke to me the other day. When the time came to make proper arrangements, she would let me have her address. Or she might communicate with me through Silk, our solicitor.

That was the note I read. It's in front of me now. No flourishes. No melodrama. Not even a suggestion of haste and generous indignation. The thing seems a whole world away from the Marjorie you and I know – or once knew. If she had simply run away – banging a door in my face, so to speak – that would be nothing: I should be looking now towards the telephone (I am writing this in the dining-room; it's nearly midnight), expecting it to ring any moment, with Marjorie, half-laughing, half-crying, at the other end, probably her sister's flat in town. But the woman who wrote that note, so cool, hostile, uncharitable, won't ring up in the middle of the night to say that we have both been very silly, that I ought to be ashamed of myself, and that she's very very sorry, and will I look out for her at Paddington at ten to twelve to-morrow morning. That I know only too well. Something's gone wrong, damnably wrong. My only consolation is that Marjorie herself disappeared some time ago, and that the exit of the writer of that note, whom I don't know, is no great matter. But no, that won't do. I shall have to think it all out to-morrow. Just now, I'm too bewildered, too tired, nothing but so many nerves and sick fancies in this hollow midnight. I'm going to bed.

It was probably the sight of your letter lying there that made me write. I opened it to see if you were still at the same address, but I haven't read it properly, only stared at it. I will leave this for the early morning post. It will be gone before I wake up and wonder why I ever wrote it.

Yours,
ROBERT.

PEARTREE LODGE,
LITTLE HURLIFORD,
OXON.

MY DEAR MARK,

   This is to thank you for your letters, especially the last, with its
Rembrandtesque interior. It is also to say that I shall be leaving here
either to-night or to-morrow morning. I shall go up to town, so until
further notice write to me at the club, the Heretics, Regency Street. You
have guessed already, of course, why I am going. Marjorie can hardly
have gone anywhere but to town, and even if she is not staying with her
sister, Doris — and I suspect she is — Doris will certainly know where she
is to be found. No, I'm not the proud tyrant of a husband suddenly
brought to his senses; this is no capitulation, no waving of the white flag;
I am going in pursuit of Marjorie — I admit the pursuit, you see — so that
we can really talk it out. We haven't done that, so far; and possibly the
fault is mine.

   She gave me the opportunity, of course, the other day when she
accused me of selfishness, egoism, and all the rest of it. You remember? I
said nothing, merely sneered in my best little donnish fashion. You will
tell me that that was all wrong, and I think now that it was. I ought at
least to have taken up the challenge, instead of pretending complete
indifference to it. No woman could forgive that. It left her with nothing
to do but leave me or climb down. I think I could have put an end to the
whole thing in a moment, always assuming that this new Marjorie, quiet
and cool and hardish, is not the real one. I could have jumped out of my
chair, thrown out my arms and cried: 'My dear, you're right and I'm
sorry! You're an angel and I've been a pig. Forgive me! — something of
that sort. Instantly, Marjorie — at least the one I know — would have
thrown her accusations to the winds and sworn that it was as much her
fault as mine. That large generosity of temper, sudden and magnificent
striking of the colours, has made me feel as small as a gnat, ashamed of
our strutting and punctilious sex, more times than I care to remember.
It's possible, of course, that this time she would not have responded; she
may see me now as an altogether different person, with whom one does
not practise such generosities; it certainly looks as if she herself has
completely changed. But if I had made the gesture, I should now know a
great deal more than I do about us. Either it would have succeeded, and

all would have been well. Or it would have failed, and I should have known at once that the old Marjorie or our old relationship was dead.

Then why didn't I make the gesture? This is the part I don't think you will understand, not exactly because you are too young (I don't often come the old 'un over you, do I?), but rather because, being still happily bemused in the moonshine and mystery stage of love, still dreaming beneath the apple-blossom of Eden, you have had no experience of this kind of relationship between a man and a woman. Well, then, if I had had a strong impulse to jump from my chair and cry to her, 'I'm sorry. Forgive me!' and so set flowing a tide of emotion that would have instantly carried us both away from these shoals and reefs, I would not have resisted it. I had such an impulse but it wasn't a strong one. I should have been merely indulging in tactics. And tactics won't do. Things have gone too far for them. They would have been disgusting, a cheap patching up. It was time for intellectual honesty – so difficult, so dangerous, so supremely necessary, between husbands and wives – to break in. A gradual estrangement of this kind isn't simply lovers' play: it means that what went before was false, a dream, or that one of you is changing, or that you are growing away from one another. It's easy enough to wave thought aside and let emotion come charging in, memories of old happiness and all the rest of it; to make it up that way and then talk it over. But I have come to see that this talking it over afterwards is rarely honest; you are too anxious to confirm your recovery of one another, to prove that the helter-skelter charge of emotion did really carry the day. No, we had to talk it out coolly, honestly.

She herself, as I think I told you, was cold and clear enough when she pointed out that I was no longer tolerable as a husband. Why, then, you will ask – or would ask if there were no Rossetts camping in your mind – didn't I meet her charges or put forward my own, in short, talk it out with her? (I am writing all this for my own benefit, not yours, giving my thoughts the test – pitiable enough – of ink and paper.) Well, I didn't because, in the first and most honest place, I was rather too bewildered, perhaps hurt. And in the second place, I felt I could only begin by making precisely the same charges, which would have sounded like the time-old 'And so are you!' But I should have meant them. It has seemed to me lately that Marjorie has been growing more and more selfish, turning herself into that awful thing, the female egoist. Of course you won't admit it. (And I'm not asking you to; this is a confession rather than a canvass.) This selfishness, this egoism of hers, are too subtle, too neatly and prettily overlaid with graciousness and charm, for you to see. They are not like some grumpy piece of bad manners, the kind of thing I suppose I can be accused of perpetrating at times. I don't intend to give you an analysis or instances: but many married women in their later thirties take to turning life into a play and themselves into limelight-haunting actor-managers, and you have to live with them, to find yourself playing Rosencrantz to their Hamlet, to be really aware of the transformation. Armed with such metaphors, I propose to seek Marjorie, though I do not imagine for a moment that I shall make use of them. But talk we must.

When two or three of us, enlightened moderns, are gathered together, how glibly we talk of our complete freedom from the foolish old conventions! I know the test now. It is this. Do we take the servants into confidence, or do we take pains to deceive them? Did Marjorie announce to them that she was leaving me? Have I announced that she has left me and that I am going in pursuit of her? You know the answer. Mrs Newlands remarked that she was going off on a short visit, and Mr Newlands has already told Mrs Birch that he too must go, being called away on business, and will let her know how long he, and possibly Mrs Newlands, will be away as soon as he can. We are frauds, you see. And we are not even successful frauds. I caught Mrs Birch eyeing me queerly when she brought in the lunch (and a bad lunch it was too – it's always the same when Marjorie's away), and I couldn't help thinking that if Marjorie had been there too, to catch that look and then exchange one with me, we would both have been suddenly shot out of this maze and have found ourselves walking together, as of old, in free air. And one thing is certain. I may discover that I can live contentedly, perhaps more contentedly, than I have lived of late, without Marjorie; but this one day has convinced me that I cannot possibly live here without her. As you know, we have not been here long – there is no question of the dear old home and so on and so forth – yet she has filled the place with her own atmosphere, and now that she has gone, this atmosphere is not that of the woman with whom I have shared a few silent meals these last few days, but of the Marjorie of an earlier time, whose ghost – with damnable unfairness – returns now to haunt these curiously empty rooms, these strange silences. This is sheer sentiment welling up. Nature, as we know, abhors a vacuum.

Tell me more about the Rossetts. I enjoy your letters, and I enjoy too the irony of these exchanges of ours. Being fellow-humans, we must really be in the same boat, but it does seem as if my end, which is leaking hard, must be a long way from yours. I won't discuss your adventures now, partly because if I draw blank in London, you may find me knocking at the door of the Brown Bull. And I promise to walk the solid ground without complaint while you tread the clouds. Meanwhile write to me at the Heretics.

Yours,
ROBERT.

P.S. – May the devil, who first thought of prosy books, fly away with the *Chimera of Romanticism*! Why am I not writing a book about real things, about apples and boats and trees aflame and hills shining in the sun? It shows what a dull fake the thing is that I simply can't think about it now.

THE BROWN BULL,
GARROWDALE.

MY DEAR BOB,

Your two letters, the brief one telling me of Marjorie's departure and its successor, leave me with nothing to say. After receiving the first I started for London, in my imagination at least. My own story seemed oddly to dwindle into insignificance and I could think all that day only of yourself. I wondered in a sort of dream what I was doing out here in a lonely valley miles away from anyone for whom I cared. Jean seemed a phantasy, beautiful, unreal, and nothing at all to do with myself. Had there been no second letter I believe that I should have left for London, but there you very rightly and wisely checked me. Your analysis of the situation was so calm, wise and right that I felt that you needed no assistance from me. My own analysis of your attitude to Marjorie seemed so crude that it appeared to me impertinent for a psychological child like myself to suggest anything. No, thinks I, up here in my northern fastness I'll stay and leave the two of them with all their older wisdom to fight it out together. So, of course, you will. And as soon as I had decided this, back Jean came again, more real and lovely and perfect than ever, and I feel the need of her quite as strongly as I did before. I suppose that your letter made me feel so childish – you have made me feel that before, you know – that I wanted to escape to someone who doesn't know me so well as you do.

In any case please let me know exactly what happens, and if you want me, I say again, send for me. I may not be much use intellectually, but at least I've got legs and can run messages. Here we've suddenly tumbled into a series of rosy crystal frozen days; everything is so still that one hears from miles away the bark of a dog, the call of a shepherd, the odd rumble that sometimes shakes the air and that is, I'm told, the blasting in a hill several miles away. The world is so beautiful at this moment that I am waiting very happily like Mr Micawber for something to turn up. It is as though if I moved I should break the spell. I have a curious certainty now about Jean; this beautiful weather has made me much more confident in some strange way. I feel the dim stirrings once more of a desire to paint, but now I want every picture to have Jean in the centre of it. Meanwhile a new light has been cast for me on the Rossett family by new friends of mine, the host and hostess of this pub, Mr and

Mrs Trump. Mr Trump is a little stout man in appearance exactly like
the pictures of H.G. Wells. Mrs Trump is a very large dominating
woman with a bosom like a sideboard and a face rather like one of
Manet's women, very black eyes and a fearless jolly expression. Mr
Trump is that rather unusual mixture, a literary publican. He is what
Wells, I imagine, might have been if he had not had any brains. Not that
Mr Trump hasn't any brains, far from it, but he has never been able to
bring them into any order. Here again he is like his famous prototype.
He has read Shaw and the R.P.A. publications and is in consequence a
desperate pessimist. Again, as with Wells, the world is in a fearful mess
because no one is thinking clearly. 'Give me six honest men who think,'
Mr Trump is fond of declaring, 'and the world will be right to-morrow.'
His suspicion of human honesty is also very characteristic of Trump; as
in the ancient cities of the plain not one honest man is to be found
anywhere. I know that he regards myself with the deepest suspicion
because I have been announced as a painter and yet have nothing to
paint with.

He has a further very interesting characteristic of seeing everybody
around him in a light exactly opposite from the accepted one. He
astonished me, for instance, immensely by confiding in me when we
were alone that the matter with Mrs Trump, whom nevertheless he
greatly admires, was that she was too mild, always giving in to
everybody when she ought to stand out, too gentle and optimistic in her
views of the human race. Well, I haven't known Mrs Trump very long,
but from the little I've seen and heard of her I would say that I have
seldom been in contact with a woman louder-voiced, more resolutely
dominating and more firmly determined that every subordinate was a
rogue and a vagabond. Also she does not, I must say, give way to Mr
Trump in any sort of weak, gentle fashion. Nevertheless, his view of her
has its success, because this morning as I was going out I heard her
giving him as sound and noisy a rating as you could wish. He listened
very quietly, and all that he said at the last was, 'Well, Naomi, it's all
right, my dear, I'll see to it. You're too amiable about these things, a
little too kind-hearted if I may say so,' which, although it must be a
game that he's been playing with her for years, seemed as brilliantly
triumphant as ever. All the wind was out of her sails, she muttered
something and went off.

In the same way he has a theory about himself that he is a kind of Jack
the Giant-killer, always knocking people about, a man of ferocious
temper and violence. I've seen no signs of the violence as yet, he is
gentleness itself with everybody and is, I am sure, feared by none, but this
theory helps him probably to get through life valiantly. I only can't
imagine how he sustains it.

We all have our illusions, of course, and I think I know some of mine, but I never could imagine myself to be a second Dempsey, another Velazquez, or a budding Lloyd George.

The interest for myself in his point of view is that he sees the Rossetts in a way that is very fascinating. I have been all this time trying to impress you with the fact that old Rossett is a violent and abusive tyrant. Trump sees him very differently. To him he is a perfectly ludicrous man, mainly, I understand, because he has no ideas. He has never thought a thing out in his life, says Trump, and there I have no doubt he is right. He goes about cursing and swearing and abusing everybody, and half the time he doesn't know what it's for. I've a kind of weakness for him myself, but I can't help laughing at him. I suggested that in spite of Trump's kindly feeling he was rather a tyrant in his own family. Well, who wouldn't be, Trump answers, with a son like that? He is crazy on his family, traces it back for thousands of years, got a Druid grandfather if all's to be believed, but after all these years what does it come to — nothing but that miserable worm poking about borrowing sixpence here and a shilling there, getting a cheap drink off anybody he can. Chloroform is what he needs. There's his daughter, I suggest. Here, again, Trump drew a picture quite other than any that I had expected. Jean apparently is his pet, his pride, and his joy, but not in the least for her looks, her gentleness and charm. He sees nothing of these things; he likes a woman, he told me, what *is* a woman, large and full, so that you don't have to look at her twice to see that she is there. No, he appreciates Jean for her ideas, the only one in the countryside apparently who has thought about anything. In his opinion she should go to London and write books about international politics. She is as clever as a man, he ended admiringly, or as a man ought to be if he ever did any straight thinking. I asked him why was it, then, that she remained shut up in this lonely valley? He told me that she'd got a kink about her father and brother. The mother having died years ago, the girl thought it was her duty to look after them and see that they didn't come to any harm. Harm! snorted Trump contemptuously, those two would come to harm if you put them in a padded cell. Her brains wasted on two mumps like that. Mump, by the way, is one of his favourite words; a mump, I gather, is something a degree lower than a chump; practically everybody is a mump. I am sadly afraid that I am already one myself. Trump's view of me by the way, is, I think, that I would make a very good middle-weight and ought to begin training for it; sport's my line, he considers — I, who have never played a game decently in my life. But, I repeat, his method has its advantages; I am beginning already to wonder whether for the purpose of rescuing Jean it wouldn't be well for me to do a little training. Maybe I'm stronger than I fancy.

Good-bye, Bob, don't take too seriously the opening of this letter. Please let me hear as constantly as you can find time for, and remember if you want me send for me.

Yours affectionately,
MARK.

P.S. – Here's fun! The elder Rossett has arrived asking for me and calling out in his jolly masterful way that I should come and have a drink with him. We shall make, who knows, an evening of it. In any case I'm going to miss no chances.

THE HERETICS,
REGENCY STREET, W.1.

MY DEAR MARK,

Your letter — filled with what we might call Trumpiana — arrived here this morning. Things seem to be at a standstill for both of us. I have heard nothing so far about Marjorie, and am beginning to think she can't have made for London after all. I am also beginning to feel very foolish. If it is idiotic — as I suggested to you it was — to follow a girl you don't know from Euston to Keswick, it is even more idiotic to go in pursuit of a runaway wife who has gone the Lord knows where. So don't talk of my being calm and wise and right, as if you were corresponding with Socrates: it makes me feel all the sillier. Consider the absurdity of my position.

I came here to find Marjorie, and the only thing I can do is to go round to all her relatives and friends who live in town. But I can't walk in, crying 'Marjorie's run away. Is she here?' I have to pretend that I am paying little duty calls, but I have no sooner arrived in the drawing-room than I am asked 'Where's Marjorie?' or 'How is Marjorie?' Then I have to mumble some nonsense or other, and very soon, if they are women, they jump to the conclusion that there is something fishy about me, and after I have been in the place about half an hour they are so sure that there is something fishy about me that I sit there feeling like a monstrous cod-steak waiting for its sauce. And even then, I don't really know whether Marjorie is there or not, because their little questions might easily be a put-up job, suggested by Marjorie herself, who is probably listening at the nearest keyhole. You know what women are. But no, you don't, unless by chance some crafty nurse still haunts the memory of your childhood.

The obvious place for Marjorie to go first was her sister's flat in Kensington. (You've met Doris, I think: she's like Marjorie, but shorter, rounder, darker, jollier, entirely without that central flame which for ever keeps Marjorie excited and exciting. She's a prose version of Marjorie. I like her and she likes me.) Off I went, then, to see Doris on the afternoon of my arrival here, two days ago. I was just in time for a late cup of tea.

'What have you done with Marjorie?' I was asked, before I could reach a chair.

'Oh, she's not with me this time——' I began, rather lamely.

Fortunately, Doris had a grievance and cut in with it. She hadn't had a letter from Marjorie for a month. Not a single line. And there were several questions that Marjorie ought to have answered long ago. Had I a message? No? It was really too bad.

I said it was too bad, and tried hard to think of some remark that would banish Marjorie from Doris's thoughts. But I wasn't quick enough.

'What are you doing with her down there?' she asked, giving me a wide innocent stare. I know that look only too well; it is really anything but innocent; and when I meet it I always call up the last reserves.

'Marjorie,' I said firmly, 'has been rather worried and very busy. She's had a visitor.' And then I drew the Masham, who makes a magnificent red herring, across the trail. Doris went after the scent, in full cry, for nearly ten minutes, while I sat there congratulating myself. Then she suddenly returned to Marjorie.

'But why didn't she come up to town with you?' she asked.

'She doesn't always, you know,' I replied. 'Don't you think it's rather absurd for a husband and wife to pay these little visits together? It's always seemed to me—— '

'Yes, Robert,' she broke in, 'I've heard you talk about that before, and I've no doubt you're perfectly right. But why shouldn't Marjorie——'

There was a noise, a blessed noise, outside. I held up my hand. Doris stopped. 'It must be John,' she said. 'He's early.'

'John, eh? Splendid!' I said loudly and cheerfully. I thought she gave me a rather suspicious little glance. She must have thought that I had grown fond of her husband very suddenly. And she had reason to be suspicious. I don't think you have ever met John Bampton, but you must have heard me talk about him. He's a solicitor and only a year or two older than I am, but in his solemn presence I feel a frivolous and flippant boy. There is nobody older than John. He has always been like that. When I first met him, about fifteen years ago, he was a Young Liberal, and even among the Young Liberals, in whom no glimmer of youth has ever been discovered, he stood out by reason of his patriarchal qualities, his earnestness, his solemnity, his dreary breadth of mind. John's mind is so broad, that everything in it loses its colour and shape. That noble white forehead goes about turning everything into a drab mush. After half an hour of his lucid talk on any subject, you feel you never want to hear about it again. If he was employed to talk to the criminal classes about robbery and murder, not another crime would ever be committed, from sheer lack of interest. I have heard him discuss the most exciting people and events and books, and have marvelled at the way in which he has left them bleached and shapeless. It is really an extraordinary gift, and I have spent many an idle moment devising uses for it. For the rest, he is kind and honourable, an ideal solicitor, I imagine, and an admirable husband and father. He would be a prominent figure in any Utopia, and I never spend an evening with him without thanking God for keeping me out of a Utopia.

But this was John's hour. I was delighted to see him, for there was not another man in London who could so readily and innocently shatter a dangerous talk about personal relations. I doubt if John realises that personal relations exist: a sub-committee is about his nearest approach to them; and I can never understand how he came to be married. (As a subject for ribald jokes, he has been meat and drink to me for years.) Well, no sooner had we shaken hands than I made a few flippant generalisations on public affairs. That was enough. He brought the full breadth of his mind to bear on these topics for the next three- quarters of an hour, during which I enjoyed my pipe and the sight of Doris's boredom. Then it was time to go, I said; and reached for my hat. No, I could not dine with them. But I did not get off so lightly. Doris told me very firmly that she was shopping in Regent Street the next morning and that I must give her lunch. I saw there was no escape.

Yesterday morning, then, we met. 'Now,' she said, before we had even given our order, 'what's happened? You and Marjorie have quarrelled, haven't you?'

I hedged for a few minutes, but saw that it was useless. Then I told her what had happened. Doris is very sensible, and I thought she would make a good ally. She distributed blame impartially – but not without a certain gusto – between the pair of us. I won't, however, bore you with that. She admitted that the most important thing to do was to find Marjorie (who was, she said, obviously in earnest this time, and ought not to be left alone), and we tried to work out a plan of campaign. She thinks that Marjorie never came to London, chiefly because she is certain that Marjorie would have gone straight to them. (I am not sure about this but didn't say so.) Her other reasons – which have more to recommend them – are that Marjorie would meet too many people she knew in town, and that she would prefer some quiet place so that she could 'think it out.' But we made a little list of people in London, an odd aunt or two and a few old friends, to whom Marjorie might have gone, and Doris thought of possible hostesses in the country and promised to write a few discreet notes and do a little telephoning. So far we have both drawn blank, and all I have had for my trouble has been some idiotic hours of calling, as I remarked before. It's possible, of course, that Marjorie is not staying with relatives or friends but at some hotel, a country or seaside hotel, I imagine; and I intend to discuss this possibility with Doris when I see her this afternoon.

I had hoped to relieve my feelings, which are of the strongest, by telling you what I think about this monstrous warren, this milch-cow of publicity men, journalists, quacks, harpies, brigands, called London, but I will bottle up my wrath. There's a limit to my powers of penmanship, the supply of club notepaper, and your stock of patience.

Yours,
ROBERT.

MY DEAR BOB,

I meant to have written to you yesterday but went off into the hills in a
strange state of ecstasy and happiness and bewilderment. I don't know
where I got to or what I did; it was one of the happiest days of my life,
but I can tell you nothing about it; I can only give you a reason for it,
which I will do in a moment.

But first a practical piece of news which concerns you. Who do you
think is staying only some five miles from here, not only staying but also
known to my drinking friend Mr Rossett, and probably, so small is the
world, very shortly to be known to myself too? Who but your own dear
spiritually minded, richly endowed Mrs Masham! There is a little valley
just over the hill – possibly you remember it – called Lambdale, and in
Lambdale there is a house with all modern improvements, hot and cold,
billiard room, garages and all sorts, called Pine House; and who took
Pine House last year on quite a long lease but Mrs Masham herself! She
was there apparently in the early summer and is known slightly to the
Rossetts; she is there again now and intends to stay apparently for some
weeks. She has a grand car, it seems, in which she once penetrated the
fastnesses of Garrowdale, suffered some motor misfortune, interviewed
my friend Trump, and finally went to the Rossetts for assistance. She had
tea there, flattered Rossett, said that he had a spiritual eye, whatever that
may be, and invited him to go and see her. Isn't the world a small place?
and how vastly more numerous are the coincidences in life than in
fiction! Now it has come to me that there is a possibility that Marjorie
may be with Mrs Masham. Why not? Mrs Masham was the outward and
visible cause of your trouble if not the inward and spiritual one, and I
think it just the kind of thing that Marjorie may have said to herself,
'Well, he doesn't like Mrs Masham, I'll show him,' and gone straight off
to stay with her. Marjorie's going as she did without a word to you is so
unlike her as I know her that I am sure that it is only a temporary piece
of melodrama; if it were serious and deep she would, I am certain, have
discussed it and considered it with you at far greater length. It is because
she knows that it is not going to last that she can make this separation a
little theatrical, she thinking it may be good for you and fun for herself. I
don't mind betting, however, that wherever she is she is already longing

for you; there is nothing like a little absence, not too severe, to make the heart grow fonder.

I am finding it, however, very difficult to write to you. Once again you have become unsubstantial to me and wraith-like. I can't even recall your features except that you have a rather long nose and a determined chin! It isn't at all your fault, everyone is like that to me now since the evening before last. I am not writing to you in fact for your benefit or amusement, but only because if I put these wonderful things down on paper they will seem more surely facts. I asked Trump yesterday morning before I went for my walk as to whether he had never, in spite of his pessimistic philosophy, felt that it was good to be alive. Yes, he said, he had once, and a very dangerous condition of things it was; he was glad that he'd got it thoroughly out of his system. He spoke of it as though it were mumps or measles. I asked him, however, what the occasion had been; I expected him to allude to his first meeting with Mrs Trump. But not at all. He said that the only occasion that he could remember when he had really felt it good to be alive was when he learnt that his father-in-law had been drowned at sea. He explained to me that he had borne his father-in-law no grudge, but that he had been both so unagreeable a man and so healthy that, taking the view of life he did, he was certain he would have the man on his hands, drinking his beer and eating his victuals, infuriating him with his drunken good-humour and his persistent cheerful borrowings, for ever and ever. The father-in-law had, however, gone to Ramsgate on a holiday, gone out in a little boat, and been drowned. On receiving the news Mr Trump had really felt that life was good; it had been, he said, a golden day. My day yesterday was also a golden day, and for reasons, I dare to fancy, better than Trump's.

But first I must tell you something more about my friendship with Rossett; that has been improving apace. It isn't that he wants me, but rather that he wants a kind of tub into which to pour a flood of drunken self-satisfied bullying egoism. I have never known in life before so insufferable an egoist. Everyone with any character is of course an egoist, and if the character is interesting enough you can forgive and even enjoy the egoism, but the most awful thing in the world is an egoist without character. Rossett has no personality; he is only a swilling, surging mess of passions, cruelties and ignorances, but with these he has the sort of pathos of an animal caught in a trap. He makes exactly the movements of something held in fierce blind pain without knowing why, indeed without knowing anything. He thinks that he is a splendid creature, a kind of Prometheus Bound, and if he can only force himself free he will do the most marvellous things. He has a contempt for everyone and everything; his flood of talk is full of anecdotes of how he got the better of this man or that. His one great quality is his love of this soil which gives him something mysterious, as though he were a tree blown in a perpetual gale or a house about to fall or a river swollen into a noisy flood feeling its power and not knowing what to do with it. I think he is growing desperate, partly because drink has sodden him, partly because he is in every kind of money mess and sees no way out of it, partly because he is really lonely with the sort of loneliness of an animal in the Zoo. I detest him and would fly from him to the farthest ends of the earth were it not for Jean, but I know that she is in increasing danger from his tempers and wildness. I have the feeling that it is not too late if someone were to take him in charge; had he money enough and a bullying truculent wife who would reduce him to order and sobriety he might turn, I think, into one of those rather fine-looking stupid and conceited old men who, when whipped often enough by a hard-hearted woman, are tamed into some kind of social decency. If I could only find such a woman, Jean would be free.

And now for the great fact of my existence. The evening before last, between five and six, on the road between here and Farthing Hall, I talked with Jean. I came upon her quite suddenly, one always seems to come upon people suddenly in this mysterious valley; she was walking quickly along and almost ran into me. As soon as I realised that it was she and saw that she was intending to pass me with a rather stiff little bow and without a word, I stood in front of her and forced her to stay. I told her that I had been waiting for days to speak to her, and speak to her I would, and then I perceived that, hide it as she might, she was glad to see me. And when I knew that, I was so happy that the road and the stream and the shadowy hills were transformed into something miraculous. I didn't lose my head, I didn't say any of the things that for days I had been preparing to say; I only, there and then, without wasting any words, told her I had loved her from the first moment that I saw her in the theatre, that I had deliberately followed her, that I wasn't ashamed of doing so, and that so long as I felt that I could be of any use to her I would stay near her whether she liked it or no, that I wouldn't bother or disturb her, but that there I was and there I would remain.

She didn't waste any words either; no nonsense about my being impertinent, that she would tell her father, that I was a rogue and a rascal, nothing of that kind at all. She simply said that I was wasting my time, that she was, as I knew, engaged to be married, that she needed no help from anyone, that she was sorry that she was late and must go on. I asked her then whether she had so many friends that she could afford to lose a good one. She replied, speaking very quickly but looking at me with a strange sort of friendliness as though she were glad in spite of herself that I had said what I had, that her life gave her no opportunity for making friends, that she thanked me very much, and hoped that I wouldn't continue to stay in so quiet a place so uselessly. I answered that it wasn't useless, and that so long as she was here I should be here too. She then said something so splendid for me to hear that I have been repeating it to myself ever since. Her words were something like this: 'It is hopeless for us to be friends; I wanted sometimes to have one, but long ago I realised that I couldn't do what I have to do except in certain conditions. You don't know anything about me, you wouldn't find me in any way interesting if you knew me better, and you mustn't know me better. But I would like to say – I have been wanting to say ever since the other night – that it was wonderful that anyone should speak to me as you did. I'll never forget it and will always be grateful to you, but please, if you feel as you say you do, if you really want to help me, don't let's meet again. If you want to help me, go away to-morrow and forget me; there's no hope at all for anything else.' Then she looked at me as though she really were seeing me for the last time and wanted to remember me. It was dark and we could only see one another with difficulty. I only said, 'What you ask is impossible, but I won't bother you, I'll only wait till you need me.' Then we parted. Now do you understand why I'm happy?

Your affectionate
MARK.

THE HERETICS,
REGENCY STREET, W.1.

MY DEAR MARK,

Your last letter is still so excited (as well it might be) that it dithered in my hand a few minutes ago. I am wondering yet, after having read it through three times, whether it tells me a great deal or tells me nothing. Take, for instance, what you call your 'practical piece of news.' Now I had thought about the Masham myself, and Doris and I, having still drawn blank here, had made up our minds to find out where she is, or at least we had made up our minds that Doris should find out where she is. I have had no news yet. And now you come with your 'practical piece.' But is your Mrs Masham – sensible enough to take a house in Lambdale – *the Masham*? If you had seen her yourself or only heard her voice booming down one of the valleys, I should know at once, that is, you would know and would tell me. But so far as I can see, you have only heard about this Mrs Masham, and the name is common enough. I can't see my Masham among the fells; they would never stand it. I am sceptical, you see. Go scouting, take a peep at Lambdale; or, if you really cannot leave the vicinity of Farthing Hall, then ask your queer friend Rossett or your Jean what this Mrs Masham is like. A word then will settle my doubts.

But even if it is the right one and the long arm of coincidence has strained its tendons, I don't imagine for a moment that Marjorie is there. I had thought of such a possibility when first I began to wonder where the Masham went to after she left us, but after some reflection I dismissed the idea. No, I am convinced that Marjorie has tucked herself away in some little hotel, and this very minute is either holding a long imaginary conversation with me (and hitting the centre of my shuddering target with every remark) or calling Three Spades on the King, Knave, and two others and one outside trick. And if this reads as if I agreed with you that she is not serious about all this, then it does not represent me fairly. I believe her to be in earnest for once. And I am serious, too, don't forget that, you romantic young loafer!

Not that you aren't – as people say – getting on. I like the sound of your Jean. To begin with, she seems about fifty years out of date, and that fact alone prejudices me in her favour. I have had the misfortune to meet and sometimes to entertain a few young damsels here who are, you might

say, bang-up-to-the-minute. Some look like a very unpleasant type of
Sixth Form boy, and some look like Brazilian moneylenders. They treat
me as I would treat a dear old lady, well past seventy and long buried in
the country. And, of course, they don't understand irony. (Perhaps I don't
understand the irony of dear old ladies – it's a chastening thought.) The
more I see of them, the more I approve of your doing your courtship in
Cumberland – or the Orkneys – or Iceland. I suppose that when these
damsels are safely wedded, they will turn into ordinary pleasant females,
but it seems incredible. Marjorie, I remember, was always able to
penetrate these fearsome disguises and to discover nice girls and the like
underneath them, but I must confess that I can't; the strange appearance,
the manners and voices, the fantastic conversation of these beings are too
much for my reason, which tries to stammer something about women
not changing in a few years but soon gives up the task of trying to
convince me. If I were told that creatures were being quietly imported
from Mars and let loose in the West End of this city, I should not be at all
surprised.

Even you, who spend so much time in town, must have noticed that
there is something very queer about it. I will tell you what it is. The
crowds get bigger and bigger, don't they? You admit that? I notice it
every time I come up. But I notice too that every time I spend a few days
here there are fewer human beings in the place. I don't suppose there are
more than a hundred human beings, real people, between Ludgate Circus
and Hyde Park Corner at this very moment. In two years' time there will
not be fifty. What is happening? Where do these crowds, so busy
shopping, dining, playgoing, come from, and of what stuff are they
made? What becomes of the real people? Are they killed and eaten?
These are sinister inquiries. There is something very queer going on in
the world. I suspect a planet-to-planet movement: creatures from Saturn
or somewhere are being dumped upon us, being shot down about four in
the morning into Piccadilly Circus; and human beings are being quietly
spirited away to Mercury or Jupiter. It may be our turn soon. If you don't
hear from me for a week or two, you will know that I too have gone,
that one morning I jumped into a rather odd-looking taxi that suddenly
made for the quietest corner of the Park and then went roaring into
space.

Three times have I been to the theatre this last week; once by myself,
once with Doris and John, and once with Mary Rounceford, who is as
sensible and charming as ever (another quarter of an hour and I should
have confided in her) and who sent you her love. When I hinted that
you were busy falling in love in the wilds, she said, 'It's all right if he
doesn't want to paint her,' which I thought very penetrating, though I
am not sure you will see the force of it. Perhaps I ought to explain that

her 'all right' meant that you would be really and truly in love. But I was talking about the theatre. All these three plays, *Horns of Truth*, *The Badger*, and *The Wise Wife*, are successes, and with these eyes have I seen solemn newspaper columns devoted to their wit and wisdom. But then you've probably seen them. You still go to the theatre a good deal, don't you? That's why I am making you responsible. Tell me this then. Why are all the characters in these plays creatures in only two dimensions, things cut out of cardboard, beings that clearly have no existence off the stage, vanishing into thin air or being packed away in boxes once they have reached the wings? And tell me this too. What happens nowadays to a man who really wants to *act*, that is, to pretend to be many different kinds of people, a tall thin melancholy parson this week and little fat jolly publican next week, and so on and so forth – does he starve? Most of the actors don't seem to play parts at all, they merely walk on; not only do they not change their personalities, they don't even change their clothes or part their hair differently; they must wonder sometimes whether they are at the theatre or in the Garrick Club. I really prefer the music-halls, though they are becoming desperately refined and no longer have an adequate supply of those large vulgar *artistes*, each with a personality, a stage presence, like a kick from a mule.

I shan't stay much longer in town. The only real heretics left in this Heretics Club are the kitchen staff, who put before you stews and dubious fishcakes from which orthodoxy would run screaming. The food they serve now is exactly suited to the tastes of those earnest rationalists who disdain all pleasures of the body because they are so fully and happily occupied persuading people that they have no souls. The next club I join will have a sprinkling of bishops and heads of colleges and other people who would not sit in the same room with a fishcake or a helping of tapioca pudding. Yesterday I lunched here with a new member, a psycho-analyst, who, apart from the fact that he is completely insensitive, rather unbalanced, and entirely humourless, is well qualified to grapple with the secrets of the human soul, to medicine us to that sweet sleep we owed yesterday.

Having had to stop writing in order to fill my pipe, I have just glanced through this letter. It seems to me a peevish and priggish affair, a performance typical of those men whose wives run away, and no sort of thing to send to a modest and engaging young man who is about to persuade a girl to run away *with* him or to fight her very unpleasant father. (And that seems to be the situation – is it?) So please forgive it and me. And don't keep me in suspense and this city much longer, but find out at once if it is really the Masham who is your neighbour, and, if it is, try to discover if she knows anything about Marjorie. You can tell her

what has happened if necessary; I don't care; I cannot feel a bigger fool
than I do at this present moment. Do that, my dear Mark, and you earn
the gratitude, not to be despised when you may elope at any minute now
and so want a confederate, of your friend

ROBERT.

THE BROWN BULL,
GARROWDALE.

MY DEAR BOB,

Funny to get your screed from London! Theatres, modern young women, crowds and the rest. Here the silence advances and advances, silence piling upon silence. One becomes slowly part of the background, a tree, a stone. I dreamt oddly enough last night that my feet had grown into the ground – near here where the stream runs. The water trickled over my ankles. I wasn't distressed. I sighed with a kind of content. Here at last all my problems were solved. London and everything in it seems useless and unreal. Jean isn't there for one thing, and for another – well, Jean isn't there.

As to my Mrs Masham of Lambdale not being your Mrs Masham, that's nonsense. Of course she is. Didn't Rossett say something to me of her being a woman of 'damned advanced ideas'? And did God ever waste coincidences? But in a day or two I'll confirm it. My affairs are moving now so swiftly that they will include Mashams and everything else very shortly. There'll be nothing left out in the world – Forster's 'Telegrams and anger' – do you remember? – Blake's linnets and tigers, the crumpled hills, Trump's stewed eels (his favourite food), Manet's 'Balcon,' and the two ladies from Liverpool now staying at this inn, artists, God help them, painting water-colours like Neapolitan ices. Everything, everything included! One day Jean will say to me (when we are sitting above the temple at Taormina looking at Etna), 'At last I know how everything is transmuted in love,' and I shall answer, 'Even to Trump's eels and Miss Maule's (Miss Amy Maule, the thin one, blue nose, chilblains, and a locket) water-colours.'

Meanwhile listen to the oddness of this. I told you that last night I dreamt that my body was rooted in this neighbouring stream. Well, the night before I had another dream. I was in a room – I see it yet most vividly, London, I think – with high windows, shabby dusty furniture, torn newspaper on the floor, an old piano, and, of all things in the corner, a harp! I was listening at the door. And on the other side of the door someone else was listening. Someone – I don't know who – was with me in the room. We were both in great danger and from the person – male or female – on the other side of the door. How vivid even after these two days! The dust, the high windows crowded with roofs, the newspaper, the harp. . . . And now listen to the coincidence!

Last night about eight o'clock I was hanging around outside Farthing Hall. Yes, hanging around, and I'm not ashamed to own to it! I had had a hunger all day to see Jean. I had hesitated as I'm always hesitating. I might simply have beaten on the door and demanded of the elder Rossett a drink, but she had asked me not to come and so I wanted an excuse that would justify myself to her. Well, I got my excuse all right.

I was standing there in the moonlight feeling an ass (a cross between a detective, a burglar and a crook-hunting policeman) when I saw the oddest figure coming up the moonlit road. Something (for it wasn't like anything human) lurching, stumbling, wavering, taking a running step or two, then almost tumbling on to its face, pulling itself back, throwing shadows like mountainous monkeys up and down. I came to meet it. It almost collapsed into my arms. It was the younger Rossett, disgustingly violently drunk. Drunk though he was he recognised me. 'Hullo, you painter fellow,' he whispered; then, lurching from me (because even in his drink he detested me), he collapsed in a heap on the road. I picked him up, pushed the gate, dragged him up the path, banged on the door. The sound echoed right through the house. It was a dead house, only the three crinkly mountains, like ancient carved animals in the moonlight, stonily watching. I waited, but as no one came I turned the heavy handle. The door opened. I pulled him into the white-flagged hall and looked about me. I swear to you, Bob, I've never been in a place so dead. The door through to the sitting-room was open, the curtains weren't drawn, the room, crammed with its odds and ends, all, as it were, with their ears cocked listening, was flooded with moonlight. Not a sound.

'Hullo!' I cried, 'is anyone there?'

The drunken swine on the floor began to call out too – hunting noises. 'Yoicks! Yoicks!' We made a fine babble.

Down the stairs came the elder Rossett. I could see that he was in a fine rage, and he crossed the hall rapidly and gave his beautiful son two beautiful kicks. He seemed to swell with anger as he stood over him. He was immense there in the moonlight with all the knick-knacks listening to him. I thought he was going to strike his son in the face. But he didn't. Without vouchsafing me a word he just picked up his offspring like a bundle of dirty washing and dragged him up the stairs. I waited, the house as silent as the tomb. But now that I was here, see Jean I would. I walked into the sitting-room and had an odd sense that as I moved forward the hills ran through the moonlight to meet me. Then on into the little dining-room, and there was Jean, quite alone, standing, her head raised, listening. She didn't seem surprised that I should be there. She only asked me quickly what the matter was. I explained – rather clumsily, I'm afraid. She broke out:

'Oh why! . . .' then stayed listening again.

I began to plead with her to let me help her. I told her that there was a fate in this, that I hadn't forced myself here but was brought by necessity. That she must know now that she could trust me. She turned to me and I saw that she was on the edge of tears. She could just hold herself in control. And that was too much for me. I had no choice. I took her, held her close to me and kissed her, her hair, her eyes, her mouth. . . . For an instant, for a miraculous heaven-blessed instant, she stayed there, then she pushed me back and looked at me – yes, I'm sorry to say – with exactly the look of hatred that her pretty young brother gave me.

She said something, called me a cad or a coward or a blackguard – I neither know nor care – when she stopped. To my amazement she put her finger to her lip, drawing me suddenly into a conspiracy with her. She even put out her hand towards me. We stood there, the two of us, frozen in the moonlight. Not a sound. I was reminded instantly of my dream. There was someone on the other side of the door. This wasn't the room of my dream, but there was the same sense of apprehension and almost terror. I can only remember now that I was triumphantly happy because, although I'd kissed her, she could still appeal to me for help. I took one step to the door and flung it open. The elder Rossett was standing on the other side of it. I had just time for an impression of real devilish malevolence. What had he seen? What had he heard? I don't know. I'm only sure that in the traditions of the best melodrama he was at once polite and amiable. Offered me a drink, thanked me for helping his son, saw me to the door, his heavy hand on my shoulder, smiled friendlily as he closed the gate behind me. I walked away under the moon. I had kissed Jean. The moon agreed that it had been a happy evening.

Affectionately,
MARK.

MY DEAR MARK,

I've had news of Marjorie at last. She spent the first two nights in town
with an aunt — but you shall have it all. I've been to Cranford and back to
gather this news.

It began yesterday morning with a telephone message from Doris, who
has developed a passion for these calls and may be murdered any night
now by the enraged club servants. Here is a slight and timid sketch of our
conversation:

DORIS. 'Good morning, Robert. Have you heard anything? No?
Then, listen — are you listening?'

SELF. (who hate standing at the club telephone). 'Yes.'

DORIS. 'It was awfully silly of me not to think of it before. I ought to
have told you to go there *at once*, the first place of all. It was stupid of me,
and I'm sorry, Robert. Are you there?'

SELF. 'Yes, yes.'

DORIS. 'It must have been because we've had a little quarrel that I
forgot about her. You know the idea? I would *want* to forget about her
and therefore *would* forget about her. Never gave her a thought, you
know——'

SELF. 'Yes, yes, yes.'

DORIS. 'But you don't know who I'm talking about, of course. Well, it's
Aunt Christina — "Teenie" we always call her — she's father's eldest sister —
very old, you know — you must have heard Marjorie talk about her——'.

SELF. 'Yes, yes, yes, yes.'

DORIS. 'Don't be so impatient, Robert. You sound quite cross. Really,
I'm not surprised at Marjorie — but, of course, you know I don't mean
that seriously——'

SELF. 'Yes, yes, yes, yes, yes.'

But need I go on? After all, I'm not trying to write a revue sketch.
The point was, that Marjorie and this Aunt Christina or 'Teenie' have
always been very fond of one another, and that Marjorie might easily
have been or still be up at the old lady's house in Highgate. 'Teenie' — or
Mrs Meldrum, as she is to the outer world — was not on the telephone,
and I ought to call at once. I told Doris that I had only met Marjorie's
aunt once — and that was at our wedding — and couldn't remember

anything about her; and I suggested that she should call. But no, she couldn't; they had had a stupid little quarrel; I would have to go myself. So she gave me the address, and yesterday afternoon I went.

By the time I had climbed to the very top of the hill at Highgate (parts of which really do look as if they were next door to Emma Woodhouse's Highbury) and had rung the bell of a little old house, I felt extremely foolish. Nor did I feel any better when I found myself in a tiny drawing-room, which seemed to be made of egg-shell, explaining who I was to a little old woman with bright blue eyes, twinkling and amiable enough, but a trifle deaf. There was also a companion – Grace Something-or-other – a neat little grey body, who sat looking at me over the top of gold-rimmed spectacles, with her hands resting in her lap and her finger-tips pressed together, and never said a word. You'd be surprised to find how trying a person can be who does nothing more than that, if you happen to be uneasy.

Well, the old lady and I chatted – or rather amiably shouted – about nothing for a few minutes. Not a word about Marjorie. Then the companion left the room, and I determined to make a clean breast of it, in spite of the fact that Aunt Christina was clearly too old for such melo-dramatic confessions.

I cleared my throat. 'The fact is——' I began.

'What's that?' She cocked an ear at me.

I had to raise my voice. It was idiotic, but there was no help for it. 'The fact is,' I yelled at her, 'I've come to inquire about Marjorie.'

'Well, I never!' Then she waited.

Now for my bombshell! 'Yes, she's run away from me.'

The old lady nodded with great satisfaction. 'I thought as much,' she said coolly. 'I knew very well she was.' Then she shrieked 'Grace,' and the companion came in again. 'She *was* running away, Grace. Didn't I tell you!'

'Dear, dear! So you did,' Grace cooed. 'Dear, dear!'

'And the obstinate girl wouldn't say a word, not a word. I knew all the time there was something.' The old lady was triumphant. 'Now please ring for tea, Grace.'

You can imagine how foolish I felt, sitting there between them. However, I learned, over tea, that Marjorie had spent the first two nights there, had sent and received several telegrams, had announced that she had invited herself to spend a few weeks with a friend in the country, and had departed early the third day.

'And now,' said her aunt, beaming at me, 'you're running after her. It's all as it should be. Wives ought to run away from their husbands sometimes – so long as there are no young children, you know – and husbands should go and find them and beg their pardon.'

'But suppose the husband doesn't feel he has done anything wrong?'

'He's always done something wrong,' she retorted. 'And what does it matter, who's in the wrong? Go and say you're sorry. You can afford it. She can't. But I know you will.'

I wasn't so sure about that, but I let it pass. 'But where did Marjorie go? Who is this friend? Did she tell you?'

Yes, she told them. And they would tell me. I sighed with relief; my idiotic search was over.

'She mentioned it just before she left,' said the old lady brightly. 'I shall remember in a minute. Dear me! How stupid of me! Mrs Sheep. No, it couldn't have been that, could it? Yet it was something about an animal, I'm sure. You remember, Grace, don't you?'

'Mrs Bean, I think,' said Grace. 'At least it was a vegetable. I'm certain a vegetable came into it.'

'Not a bit of it, my dear. I remember distinctly that it was something to do with an animal.'

'Animal, mineral or vegetable,' I murmured. 'We shall have to get that settled.'

'You see,' the old lady went on, 'it's over a week ago, nearly a fortnight, isn't it? You should have come before. You might have known she would come here at once. But doesn't this suggest anything to you?'

I thought of animals and vegetables, but could make nothing of it. Then I asked them if they remembered where she was going. That would tell me something.

'Derbyshire, I think,' said the old lady dubiously, and looked at Grace.

'Dartmoor it was, I'm sure,' Grace replied, equally dubiously, and looked at me.

This put me off the scent. We have a friend or two in both places, though I don't think Marjorie would be likely to stay with them at present. However, I tried them with a few names, without success. Then I bethought myself of your great discovery. 'Was the place Lambdale, in the Lake District?'

It was. They were excited at once. Did I know the name of the friend? I gave them Masham. That was it. And then they both spent the next quarter of an hour explaining to me how and why they thought of animals and vegetables. This at end, I made my escape.

I think there is no doubt whatever that Marjorie did leave here to go to her Masham in the very next valley to yours, though of course she may not be there now. That, my dear Mark, is what you have got to find out for me. If she is there now, I leave town at once for Keswick, and you may expect me at the Brown Bull. There is certainly no sense whatever in my staying here now, but naturally I don't want to set off on a wild goose chase. So let me know at the earliest possible moment.

It's rather selfish of me to press you in this way when your own affairs seem to be reaching a crisis. I keep wondering what is happening to you now, after that strange episode in your last – and exceedingly good – letter, though I suspect you are developing a rather Wuthering Heights-ish imagination in your lonely dale. I cannot understand your Jean yet, and I wish you would make her talk a little. When you are fat and forty and dieting (and all this will happen to you, Mark), her talk will matter most. And I don't mind telling you that I miss Marjorie's talk damnably, though that doesn't mean that I will pay any price to have it again. But it means – among other things – that I am sick of other middle-aged asses in clubs. The fact is – and nobody notices it – everybody has to marry somebody or something in this life. I have known men who were married to collections of minor eighteenth-century verse or old Italian engravings.

Yours ever,
ROBERT.

                                                      THE BROWN BULL.
MY DEAR BOB,

I was delighted to get your letter by yesterday's second post. I have
news for you, although not the final news that you want – patience, my
dear friend, all in good time. It amuses me, I must confess, to hear you
say: 'If she is there I leave town at once for Keswick.' Well, well, times
change and manners too. Who would ever have supposed that the
comfortable, well-satisfied, happily married Robert Newlands of a week
or two back would now be racing about England in search of a wife?
Will it be good for Marjorie to know of your urgency? Won't she have
the whip-hand of you for ever after? When you are together again I
should keep mum about it if I were you.

Meanwhile in my affairs you ask me to give you more of Jean's
personality, some of her talk. As to her personality, she is still a dream. As
to her talk, there has been none. I have kissed her once, exchanged ten
words. I can only tell you that with every hour I love her more deeply.
Yes, with every hour, for I find when I wake in the morning that I love
her with just seven hours' more depth than I did the night before. But
what do I love? Her hair, her eyes, the curve of her hand, the softness of
her voice? Like all lovers these, but beyond them a dream. The day will
come when I shall be in contact with reality. I shall know then whether
there is something true here. Your curiosity shall be satisfied.

Meanwhile for more tangible things. I'm writing this letter in my little
room to-night after two very strange little conversations, and one of them
closely concerns yourself. This morning I was late. Frankly I'd been lying
in bed reading *Arabia Deserta*, and it is the effect of that odd work to
carry you, if you care for it at all, so absolutely out of your own world
that deserts and strange moons and coloured carpets are your only wear.
So I was late and came stumbling down the stairs feeling the chill air of
the October morning, in my nostrils the mingled scent of bacon, boot
polish and chrysanthemums. I walked into the road shaking Arabia from
my back, and there straight in my path was a big Sunbeam, several grand
people inside it, and a chauffeur with silver buttons, and, walking very
majestically towards the Brown Bull, a stout self-pleasured woman. I say
'self-pleasured' because it was obvious that she felt that she owned not
only the car and the people in it but the Brown Bull, the road, the fields,
the hill, and God's good air.

'I'm damned,' says I to myself, 'if you shall own me or my *Arabia Deserta.*'

She approached me as though she were Queen of Sheba deigning to notice the Fifty-fifth Eunuch.

'Do you happen to know if Mr Trump's about?' she asked in a deep voice like a drum.

'No, I don't,' I answered shortly.

'I wonder if you'd tell him that Mrs Masham would like to see him for a moment?'

'Too busy, I'm afraid,' I said, preparing to move on. My indignation was only equalled by my excitement. *Your* Mrs Masham now *my* Mrs Masham and nastier than ever you painted her!

'Oh, I'm so sorry!' she boomed at me, blushing like a young bride. 'I'm always doing things like that. I'm so absent-minded that I never see people at all. I've been *so* rude.'

I assured her that she had not (for your sake, dear Bob, I must not let her go), smiled at her, said that I did not mind at all searching for Mr Trump – and then at the very moment the bucolic Wells trots forward.

He'd been watching, I've no doubt, from behind a window. The two greeted one another like old dear friends. Mrs Masham boomed, Trump guttered, and I stood there feeling foolish, while the citizens of the Sunbeam seemed to have been transferred straight from Madame Tussaud's renovated waxworks. Mrs Masham was terribly glad to see Mr Trump and hoped that he was all right and Mrs Trump very well, although she wouldn't think of bothering Mrs Trump just now and wouldn't come in, thank you, because she was showing some friends the valley, and had really only stopped to take back with her two of the books that she'd lent Mr Trump a month or so back, and if Mr Trump hadn't finished them she'd return them to him very shortly, but Mrs Carslake-Pyle who was staying with her just at the moment hadn't read either *Where is the Light?* or *The Voice from the Ether*, and was most anxious to do so, and *if* Mr Trump had finished with them——

Mr Trump *had* apparently finished them and he must say that he would have benefited from them more had they not been so light and frivolous in tone. This evidently took for the moment all the air out of Mrs Masham's drum. Frivolous? Well, no, she certainly hadn't looked on them in that light. Frivolous? But Trump was not to be shaken. Very gloomily he suggested that Mrs Masham should look into them again, suggesting, I couldn't but feel, that Mrs Masham herself was of so light and airy a build, both physically and spiritually, that if she didn't take care she'd be off floating into the air like a piece of thistledown.

Then, most unexpectedly and for what reason I don't know, he introduced me – Mr French, staying at the Brown Bull, a famous artist.

We got on then like a house in flood. I was determined that we should. While Trump was indoors fetching the books we discussed Ouija Boards, The Higher Light, The Lower Synthesis, The Utter Calm, The Radiant Soul, The Belching Will, The Aspiring Fire, and all the time the Sunbeam Upper Ten stared like mummies through the glass and thought, I've no doubt, murderous thoughts.

I'd just agreed with Mrs M. that life was nothing if it wasn't high (like a mere partridge on the kitchen fire so to speak) when I secured my invitation. Wouldn't I do her the honour of paying her a visit? No distance, no trouble, tea and Higher Thought and a meeting with Mrs Carslake-Pyle, who is rich enough apparently to keep two paid mediums always at her side. (Great thought. Who knows but the citizens of the Sunbeam are all hired mediums? That would account completely for their static pose.)

Trump returned with the books, gracious farewells were said, the invitation repeated and accepted, and the Sunbeam hurled itself into space.

Trump made but one comment. 'The matter with her is,' he said, 'she's too gay.'

Now as to the other. Very brief. Very queer. I had just come in from an afternoon stroll (in the neighbourhood of Farthing Hall, I'll confess), when there was a knock on my door and Trump poked his head in to know would I see Mr Rossett for a moment. Which Mr Rossett, I asked. The younger one.

Yes, I would, I said, my curiosity rising fast. A moment later the younger Rossett was in my room sucking, like a very youth out of Dickens, the knob of a riding whip. I didn't ask him to sit down, I didn't offer him a drink. I waited.

He scowled but was apparently anxious to be friendly. He muttered something about my helping him home the other night (what a sickly, yellow-livered, chinless young ruffian it is!) then drove himself towards his main business. He was in the devil of a hole. I'd been decent to him the other night. He was in the devil, yes, the *devil*, of a hole. Could I help him?

I stared at him blankly. He didn't know where to turn. His father (and here his countenance took an extra yellow sheen) must know nothing about it. I asked him then was it money? Yes, he said, it was – part of it. Would I lend him, just for a week or two, a little? Would I lend him two hundred pounds?

The impertinence of that took my wind. He saw that I was astonished and then with a most evil attempt at a would-be confidential grin he said – wasn't I sweet on his sister? If I were – and everything was square between gentlemen – if I'd give him a leg-up, why, he'd give *me* one.

I rose and – he fled. That was all there was to it. One glance at me and he was out of the door and down the stairs. I heard the inn door bang behind him. Well, what do you say to that? Isn't that a charming brother for my Jean to have? And aren't I getting properly caught into the Rossett affairs? I must stop. This has been long enough. Wait but a day and you shall know whether Marjorie is in Lambdale or no.

Affectionately,
MARK.

P.S. – Later. I've just had a miraculous hour with Jean. Here in this very room. I'll write to-morrow. My luck – my incredible luck.

THE HERETICS,
REGENCY STREET, W.1.

MY DEAR MARK,

I am answering yours at once, for two reasons. The first is that I want
to give you a piece of my mind. (Why is it we only give away the
unpleasant pieces?) Let me quote a few sentences from your last letter:
'Will it be good for Marjorie to know of your urgency? Won't she have
the whip hand of you for ever after? When you are together again I
should keep mum about it if I were you.' Do you think you are writing
to Bishop Proudie? Is this your notion of the married state? — whip
hands? — keeping mum? You can sit there, among those glorious hills,
pretending to be in love, and yet write so knowingly, so vulgarly, about
the most subtle and most delightful of human relationships — it is
incredible. If this is what you are in the green leaf, what will you be in
the dry? Shall I tell you why you can write such stuff to me and yet rave
like Romeo in the very next paragraph? You give yourself away when
you talk of me as 'the comfortable, well-satisfied, happily married Robert
Newlands.' At the back of your infantile mind is a conviction that
Marjorie and I are not real people, are quite different from you and your
Jean. You really imagine that when a man and a woman go to the altar or
the register office, they are changed in the twinkling of an eye, and that
after that they automatically become 'comfortable, well-satisfied, happily
married.' No such people exist except in the minds of infants. And you,
my dear Mark, are an infant.

The second reason I write at once is to point out that I am still
haunting this club (where they are beginning to hate me) waiting for
news of a woman of my acquaintance. Her name — surprisingly enough —
is not Rossett: it is Newlands, Marjorie Newlands. She is a woman in her
thirties, with brown hair of a reasonable length, grey eyes, a freckle or
two, and a small but very witty nose. Her voice — should she condescend
to speak to you — you will discover is most musical and merry, and full of
inflections that you cannot possibly hope to understand until you are
about forty. She has been very well (that is, expensively) educated, but
has had the decency to forget all about it. She regards life as a comedy,
with little romantic interludes, and is perhaps rather apt to see herself as
the producer of the particular piece in which she is taking part. I suspect
that she has more sense, real downright horse-sense, than you and I (and

I know not how many Rossetts and Trumps) put together; but on the other hand, being entirely feminine, she does not see eye-to-eye with us, and can at times be surprisingly insensitive and unscrupulous. She is a trifle suspicious of men and their little ways, chiefly because her father was a tremendous old egoist, and she stayed long enough with him to find him out. (And now, of course, you are saying that she has stayed long enough with me to find me out. Possibly. But you ought to have known the old man, very charming and inclined to be wistful, but rotten selfish, as hard inside as a battleship.) She is far more indulgent towards women, though she dislikes their hundred-and-one little barriers and fences and their silly scrapping, and really prefers the company of men. She is very, very civilised, probably about two thousand years ahead of us, but rather likes being quietly elemental: she could be a tree but not a monkey. Her sense of humour is magnificent, but has strange bare patches, so that there are times when everybody is amused, but she is disgusted or indignant, though there are still more times when everybody is disgusted or indignant and she is amused. Nothing in a newspaper ever takes her in except the advertisements of foreign hotels. I would rather have her remarks about public windbags than anybody else's. At the same time she frequently goes wrong because she does not understand how often men deceive themselves, and so mistakes a fool for a rogue. When she does discover a simple fool, she is quite happy for a time in his or her company. (Probably she sees a simple fool in Mrs Masham.) What she certainly does not understand, and never will understand, is the force of an idea and the attraction there can be in four-square consistency, the stout walls of dogma. Her nimble and subtle intelligence detests principles and codes and systems, and she is really a mental anarchist. The result is that law and order, which must come in somewhere, have it all their own way with her in everything else, and I never knew anybody so intelligent and tolerant who disliked Bohemianism as much as she does. But there again, she – but what is this stuff?

Hang it! – I was beginning to write in sober earnest. It must have been the (to me) amusing formal style that lured me on. You were very brave about the Masham. And you will be braver still if you do go to the Dark Tower itself and face not only a Masham, but a double-mediumed Mrs Carslake-Pyle, and apparently a whole astral-body house party. Really I can't see Marjorie in the middle of such a gang. (But if she is, it serves her right. I'd like to go and grin at her every night through the drawing-room window.) She probably left days ago. Let me know as soon as you can. I'm all impatience to get away from here. Your own affairs seem to be in a very queer trim.

Yours,
ROBERT.

THE BROWN BULL.

MY DEAR BOB,

This is only a note, partly to quiet your impatience, and partly to tell you that anything may happen at any moment – to me, to Jean, to the universe.

I had meant to write to you at some length about my long talk with Jean last night. But now I can't. For one thing matters are too serious; for another – well, for another, I can't let myself go to anybody, not even to you.

She came to ask whether I'd been lending money to her beastly brother, and if I had I wasn't to. I said I hadn't. Then I let go, told her that I could endure this no longer, help her I must whether she liked it or no. She was on the edge of her own endurance, I think, and quite suddenly began to tell me everything as though we'd been friends a thousand years. Everything? It didn't after all amount to very much. What it came to was that, in her estimation of herself, she'd failed altogether to fulfil the one duty that life had given her – to look after her father and brother. Things had simply gone from bad to worse. Her father was head over ears in debt, was half mad with anxiety and worry. (That's the way *she* put it – with drink and arrogance would be my version.) As to the chicken-faced brother, he'd got into some mess in London (about a thousand messes, I should think), was only drinking and wasting his time up here – and the quarrels between father and son have been apparently terrifying. What troubled her most, though, was that neither of them would tell her anything. Farthing Hall is apparently a place of mystery, no one telling anyone anything. She's out of her wits as to what to do, but her chief fear apparently is lest her brother should return to London, where the company he keeps is, it appears, devastating.

At last it came out that she had the idea that I might be of some help here, might be a friend to him (a *friend* to him! ye gods!) and persuade him to stay here. Then, after this, at long last, a confession – that she couldn't abide this gentleman farmer to whom she was engaged, and that, especially of late, the idea of marrying him had become more and more impossible. (Especially of late? Can I take any flattering unction to my soul there?) I asked her what kind of a man he was, but she could tell me nothing, he seemed to be a sort of ghost to her. I can't describe to you possibly, Bob, how simple she was in all this, how naïve and inexperienced, and yet how determined and courageous and single-minded. What am I to say more? The result of that hour last night is that I am in a state of feverish anxiety and uncertainty. Last night I slept not at all, and all day I have been in a mumbling, fuzzy, spider-web condition, when nothing is clear, nothing is real, nothing certain. Hence this stupid letter to you. All I know is that I must help her, and that soon.

Yours,
MARK.

THE HERETICS,
REGENCY STREET, W.1.

MY DEAR MARK,

I spent a good part of yesterday helping a certain Board of English Studies to set examination papers. I had promised to do so some time ago, had the note reminding me forwarded from Peartree Lodge, and had to set out at once. Thus I have actually done some work (though of the meanest kind) on this absurd trip. And while I am in the vein, I propose to set you a paper. This is it.

1. What personages are always described in the newspapers as (a) 'laughing heartily'; (b) 'looking very fit'; 'not a bit the worse for——?' Maximum marks – 20.

2. What happens to a neglected wife on the stage who does not possess a former lover, just back from big-game hunting? Maximum marks – 30.

3. 'The member for East Dulton is probably the only man in the House who still wears a black tie with red spots' – extract from Gossip Page of daily paper. Who cares about this, and why? Maximum marks – 40.

4. Mr Edwin McIghbro, who writes little reviews of novels for *The Community*, has just declared that he cannot read Fielding, Scott, Dickens, Thackeray, Trollope, and that such writers are only fit for schoolboys. Describe the state of mind of this critic on finding himself confronted by any one of these writers in person. You may give only one or two of his witty snubbing remarks, if any. Maximum marks – 50.

5. 'It should be realised that the advertising expert of to-day is performing a noble service for the public.' Explain the nature of this service, and say why it is nobler than that of a tripe-dresser or a vendor of roast chestnuts. Maximum marks – 75.

6. Why are young artists in their middle twenties and donnish men about forty so conceited? (See their correspondence.) What have they done that they should be so cocky? Maximum marks – 250.

7. WHERE IS MY WIFE? Maximum marks – 1000.

The answer to the last need not be your own unaided work. But I want it quickly. Indeed, I shall probably return to Little Hurliford tomorrow afternoon, unless, of course, I have news from you between now and then.

Yours for about 48 more hours,
ROBERT.

THE BROWN BULL.
DEAR BOB,

Marjorie is here and at Mrs Masham's; I have just had tea in her company. Partly to oblige you, and partly to get some of the restlessness and anxiety out of my brain, I hired a Ford from Trump and bumped over to Mrs Masham's this afternoon. The weather and the country fitted my mood. It's been pouring all day, there's mud on the ground, mud in the air, mud in the sky. The trees are like Macbeth's witches, and every shake of their boughs is a bad omen. However, you don't want to hear about the weather, I can see you cursing, skipping this bit and coming to Marjorie. So we clattered and slithered over to Lambdale and found our way to the hideous dwelling-place that contains fittingly Mrs Masham. It's one of those square squat white houses with chimneys stuck on anywhere, as naked as your hand and plumped down into the middle of a lot of green lawns like a Victorian novel in Bloomsbury. I rang the bell and was driven into the midst of them, having tea in the hall like a Nonconformist chapel. Marjorie was the first one I spotted, standing by the fireplace, a tea-cup in her hand, looking, you'll be glad to hear, ineffably bored. And by Jove she jumped when she saw me, she nearly dropped the tea-cup, and she took quite half a second to recover her calm, and you know that's a lot with Marjorie. You'll be pleased to hear that she is looking extremely well and very beautiful. I have never in my life seen her so handsome, or that may be by contrast, because she was surrounded by such a collection of freaks as was never seen outside a modern novel. She not only looked well and handsome, she looked also defiant as soon as she'd pulled herself together. I imagine that she thought at first that I'd been put by you on to her track, and I saw at once that she was determined to be gay and bright and very happy so long as I was there. To be gay in that crowd was no light task. Mrs Masham swallowed us all as the whale swallowed Jonah. She has the most amazing gift, that woman, of taking it absolutely for granted that people only exist because of herself; if she wasn't there we wouldn't be there either. Even the tea that we were drinking we were drinking inside her, so to speak. However, she was really very glad to see me, I think. She was orating when I came in to an attentive audience of four, Marjorie and a woman like a wedding cake, a man like one of the minor prophets disguised as Henry Irving, and a little woman like an exclamation mark. I never to the end of my visit discovered their names, so you must take them at that. Mrs Masham talked all the time that I was there, and none of the audience said anything except the little woman, who kept interjecting 'Well, I never!' 'You don't say!' 'Fancy that now!' and 'Isn't it quaint?' Mrs Masham was busy telling us all about the new doctrine of imagining yourself, when you are sick or in trouble, some sort of a plant. I didn't get the whole drift of this because I came into the middle of it, but I gathered that if you had a bad toothache and thought yourself a nasturtium, your pain would vanish. Everything depends apparently on choosing the right kind of plant for the right kind of malady; toothache nasturtium, stomach-ache pansy, sore throat sunflower (I have always detested sunflowers, and now I know why), and so on. But further than that, if it's a really bad trouble, like your wife running away for instance, a whole bunch of flowers is necessary. Pansy, violet, geranium seems to be one of the best cures. I listened to this twaddle for some twenty minutes, and took furtive glances at Marjorie meanwhile. It would have rejoiced your heart to have seen the look of contempt in her soul which her face endeavoured to hide. You're having your revenge all right if you want it. On the other hand, I will bet you a dozen of my best paintings against one of your own most unintelligible works, that she won't be able to stand it here very much longer, and that if you want to catch her, you'd better come quickly.

Well, to my muttons, or rather to yours. I never got near her until just at the last. After a long while the Masham drew breath, and we all moved into a kind of cemetery supposed to be a drawing-room. I got a few words with her as we went in. 'Well, Knight-Errant!' she said with just that mixture of raillery, mockery and affection that, if you'll forgive me for saying so, I adore her for. 'What are you doing up here?' I asked as though I hadn't heard a thing. 'Oh, just lazing,' she answered, 'and improving my mind,' she added maliciously. 'How's Bob?' I asked lightly. 'Oh, very well,' she answered just as lightly; 'haven't you heard from him?' 'A line or two,' I said; 'when he's in London he hasn't time to write much.' That struck her, she jumped all over. 'Dear Bob,' she replied, 'he does love to be busy, doesn't he?' That was every word that we exchanged, but I could see that she was tremendously stirred, that she wanted to ask me a thousand questions, that she wished the whole of that company in Timbuctoo. I could see too that she is changed, something has happened to her. I don't believe, although this is, of course, all guess-work, that you'll find your job quite so easy as you fancy, but that she longs to see you again, I'll swear.

If you're coming up, don't reckon on me. Anything may happen in my affair, and God! how I wish that it would.

Yours affectionately,

MARK.

THE BROWN BULL.

DEAR BOB,

This is the merest line to warn you that the next twenty-four hours may see me gone. This morning an extraordinary scene occurred here. The elder Rossett burst into my room to demand of me what I had done with his son. He was in an extraordinary state of rage and confusion; he scarcely seemed to see me at all but to be moving like a madman in a maze of his own. I said that I had done nothing with his son; why should I? He stormed about the room, knocked a chair over, swore that he'd kill the boy if he found him, that he'd done with him for ever, that he'd murder him, and that I was to let him know at once where he'd gone to. I said that I hadn't seen him since the day or two before, when he'd rushed in here for two or three minutes and rushed out again. What had he come here for? He'd come to borrow money. Had I lent him any? No, I hadn't. He then broke into an extraordinary soliloquy; I can't give you any idea of it except that the Deity figured in it a great deal, that he was betrayed by his children, that 'They' were all after him, but that he'd be up to them yet and give them a knock or two, that God was trying to tear him away from the one spot of ground that was his, but that every stick and stone, every river and tree and hill would resist God's efforts, that the moon was in a new quarter, and that his house was crumbling about him. Honestly that's what it sounded like, and I haven't the slightest notion what it was all about except, of course, that his pigeon-faced son has departed. Gone to London, I should fancy. What next? I don't know except that Jean is alone in that house with her crazy papa and that I've got to step in and do something about it. So don't count on me in any way whatever; all I promise is that if I leave here I'll wire to you.

Yours,
MARK.

PEARTREE LODGE,
LITTLE HURLIFORD,
OXON.

MY DEAR MARK,

Your little note, the one sent to 'quiet my impatience' (it didn't succeed), only arrived here this morning, having had to be forwarded from the club. There may be another letter from you, really giving me some news, at the club this minute, waiting to catch the eye of the clerk. The thought is maddening. However, it's my own fault. I came to the conclusion that nothing could be worse than hanging about in London. I was wrong. (And I am beginning to suspect that I am frequently wrong, which isn't pleasant.) It is much worse hanging about down here.

At the first rush I was glad to be back. There is still some real air here, and the moment I took a deep breath of it I realised that I had virtually been living for the past fortnight or so in a motor-car engine. It was fine to taste sweet air again. And then I was coming back to my own place.

But it isn't my own place, you see. It was our place, and more Marjorie's than mine. The ghost of happiness walks these rooms. I don't think I have ever spent a more melancholy two and a half days than these I have had here since I came back. The very days themselves, of course, have had to lend a hand in fixing my mood. You never saw more melancholy weather: shifting grey skies with occasional dull yellow patches over the distant Downs, sudden gusts of wind stripping the trees and piling up dead leaves in every corner, and now and then a cold lash of rain. It's Autumn without her usual gold, a sad bankrupt. The gardener is busy quietly taking the last traces of summer out of the garden, leaving only a few nodding desperate roses.

The house doesn't seem the same. I can't say what exactly is wrong with it, not having an eye for these details, but I suppose really it is because the maids are not doing their work properly now and a hundred and one little things are suffering from neglect. I only get the general impression, but if Marjorie were here, she would know what was wrong. It seems to me that houses are useless if they have no women queening it in them. They are too civilised for men left alone. We are only fit for barracks or colleges. I can't stay here without a wife.

But all that is little or nothing, being only part of the mere mechanics of living. These things don't hurt. But now that I am back here again, this absurd quarrel and separation of ours isn't absurd any longer. It's just as if a different set of lights had been switched on. But the change of background makes a difference. I don't see this quarrel now against a background of Doris and John, and Aunt Christinas, and clubs full of comfortable Heretics, and the nonsensical lights of Piccadilly Circus. I see it against these empty skies and black nights and – somewhere behind these – the further background of memory.

You see, being here, alone and unable to forget myself in work, try as I may I cannot help thinking of our first coming here. It wasn't so long ago, as you know, but it happened that when we took this house and began a rather different kind of life, Marjorie and I had seen, stretching out before us, an even better future than we had imagined for some time. I don't mean that we had just patched up a quarrel or anything of that kind, but that we had just reached another and finer level in our relations. This is what happens in real marriage, and that is why all this talk of settling down – as if marriage was a sediment in the medicine bottle of life – is so pernicious; it both cheapens and falsifies the thing. What happens – as I am hoping you will soon discover for yourself – is that the two of you are for ever meeting, losing one another, coming closer, meeting again, on different levels. Well, it happened that our coming here was at a time when we were unusually close together and happy, and it seemed as if we had only to do the day's work and then to sit in these rooms and this garden and talk the years away together, to bite the apple of life through to the core. All this I remember, and of course not in such stupid summarised form as this, but in all its ironic details, the smiles across the table, the last quiet remarks over the fire. And now——

If I were younger or sillier, I might imagine that Marjorie had stumbled upon the wrong man and I upon the wrong woman, and that we had perhaps only to nose about in a few drawing-rooms to find other people and so put everything right. But I know that for me at least – for I cannot speak for her – there is no such dubious consolation. If I cannot make Marjorie reasonably happy nor she me, then for me something has broken for ever. You remember what Conrad said somewhere: 'We live as we dream – alone'? I wander through this house, walk out to the decaying woods and back, with that sentence – and it's a sentence in every respect – knocking stonily in my mind. There have been times when it seemed as if I neither lived nor even dreamt alone, and now I wonder if that is only the last and greatest of the illusions that must go, if man and woman can indeed only exchange a kiss or two in the dark and then stare at one another in the daylight, shrug their shoulders and turn away. I feel now that there is nothing left for me to do but to make one last effort to put things right, and then, if that fails, to add the whole tale of love to the heap of old happy fairy-tales, the picture books, so wonderful once, that now lie tattered and mouldering in our lumber rooms. I can live without Marjorie, but the world I shall live in will not be the one I once saw stretching out before me. Perhaps that's what happens: the world narrows and narrows until at last it is no bigger than the grave into which we shall go. But no, I don't believe that.

I prefer to believe that I'm a damned fool who happens to be still in love with his wife and is beginning, just beginning, to eat his heart out because she's walked away from his foolship. And I am not enjoying my meals (very bad); there is nobody here I want to talk to; and the leaves are flying through the air. The moment I have definite news – and I live for the postman now – I shall shut up this house or leave the gardener and his wife to look after it, and be off by the next train. Inaction is the curse of this life. All the great pessimists, I suspect, were fellows who never stirred. Write to me at once.

Yours ever,
ROBERT.

DEAR BOB,

If this is incoherent you must forgive it. I don't know that I shall ever send it. I am writing directly after the event in order that it may be exactly recorded. I'm sitting down to my table with a nose that has been deluging blood, an eye half closed, and a bump on my forehead larger, I'm sure, than a football. In spite of a stiff neat whisky I'm still very shaky, as you'll see, if you ever get this, from my writing. I'm going to give you nothing, I hope, but bare facts, or, at any rate, my impression of the bare facts.

I told you in my last hurriedly scribbled note, I think, how Rossett Senior rushed into my room, gabbled some incoherencies about his son, the new moon, God and the Devil, and rushed out again. Well. This evening I found this note on my table. Simply this:

'Will you do this for me? Go to London, find my brother and help him. Don't let him know that I asked you. He goes almost every night to the Dolphin night-club in Hare Street. I've thought of every possible way, and I have no one to help me. If you hadn't said what you did last time I wouldn't have dared. Things are getting beyond me. You've made me trust you as I've never trusted anybody. . . .'

The dots stand for some words that I can't read. They are blotched over as though she had been suddenly interrupted. I can't make you understand without showing you the letter what a sense of distress and crisis it gave me. More than it need perhaps. I don't know. Probably I shall never know, but I've been so strung up and uneasy these last days that I'm no judge any more of the truth of anything.

Anyway, after I'd tried to swallow some supper and failed and walked my little room like a lunatic a hundred times, I could endure it no longer and started off up the moonlit road. Everything was dead black and white, and as still as the inside of a button. I don't know what I intended to do. I don't know that I had any intention at all, but five minutes later I was walking up the cobbled path and banging on the heavy black door.

Rossett opened it himself. He was in a dressing-gown and pyjamas, although it was only about nine o'clock, and the house behind him was as still and silent as it always damnably is. I was so surprised to see him dressed like that, or rather undressed (it made me feel suddenly shy and polite, as though I must apologise to him for knocking him out of bed), that I couldn't say a word. The moonlight fell full on him, and gave him an odd gigantic appearance as though he were nine foot high and made of marble.

'Well, what do you want?' he said. What *did* I want? I didn't know. I couldn't think of a thing except his blue silk dressing-gown and his handsome chest. He seemed to hypnotise me.

'I want to speak to you,' I answered feebly.

He motioned me in without a word. I went past him into the sitting-room. The curtains weren't drawn. The hills were staring in, and the moonlight splashed all over the floor making all the knick-knacks look as unreal as anything.

'Well, what do you want?' he asked again.

I'll confess to you, Bob, quite frankly, that I was terrified. I may as well warn you before we go any further that I haven't played a very fine part in this little scene. He looked ferocious. His chest was bare and every black hair on it seemed to threaten me. I burbled some nonsense. Then he said something like this:

'You've been plaguing me for weeks. I'm sick of you. You persuaded my son to run away, and now you're trying to seduce my daughter. Get out.'

That made me mad. I shouted something at him about his being a beastly father and a dirty blackguard, and then he went for me. He knocked a table over and all the knick-knacks tinkled to the floor. It wasn't a dignified affair. He caught me round the waist and we crashed to the ground together. Oddly enough I was on top. What odd things you notice in a scrap! I was trying to shove my knee into his naked belly, and staring beyond him, summoning all the force I had (which wasn't very much), I was looking into a ridiculous Victorian Chinese Pagoda affair, broken in half, with a green mandarin nodding his head at me. I remember that mandarin more vividly than anything else in the affair. I hadn't much time to think, though. Rossett had thighs thicker and harder than iron, and he heaved himself up and flung me off him. My nose was bleeding and that made me angry. I got to my knees, and had just time to duck before he got me with a large pink and green china vase, which just missed my head and smashed into the wall. We both got to our feet together. I don't know where the blue dressing-gown had vanished to, but his pyjama jacket was on the floor, and he hadn't a stitch on except the legs of his pyjamas that were clinging to his ankles. Looking back now it seems to me that the funniest thing I ever saw in my life was his kicking his heels to get clear of the pyjamas, dancing all amongst the broken china with the moon shining upon him. Talk of a bull in a china shop! He wasn't in very good condition, I imagine – otherwise he'd have smashed me up. But he stood there for a moment, his belly glistening with sweat, his chest heaving. Then he leapt a fallen chair and hurled himself at me. I couldn't keep a hold on him; he was slippery with sweat, so I clutched at his hair, and then we rocked about, china and stuff falling all over the place.

Then I felt my senses going. I couldn't see a thing. I thought the three hills were coming dancing into the room, the moon on top of them, and there was a great roaring in the room (I was pressed up against his heart and he was breathing like a grampus). I tried to catch on to his thigh but couldn't hold him. I thought I was going to die. His eyes were staring into mine and the end of his nose twitched in the oddest way. I remember that, because noticing it was what saved me. I couldn't stand its twitching and so caught hold of it. I'd got something I could hold on to at last, and with my other hand I just pushed at his mouth.

To my amazement he suddenly gave, just sank to the ground. I was myself on top of him. I lay there a moment holding on to his naked slippery arm. We lay there quite quietly like friends, and I heard the water from a turned-over vase of flowers dripping on to the floor. Then I pulled myself up. He wasn't dead. He lay there, grunting a little. I picked my way out over the broken china – and here I am. A ridiculous scrap. He was probably drunk. I don't know; I'm too damned tired for anything.

MARK.

Telegram from
  MARK FRENCH
to
  ROBERT NEWLANDS.

Leaving this morning for London.

MARK.

Telegram from
  ROBERT NEWLANDS
to
  MARK FRENCH.

Your Marjorie letter just arrived. Joining you to-night. Meet last train Keswick if possible.

ROBERT.

THE BROWN BULL.

MY DEAR MARK,

Could anything be more absurd than this? I spent last night in the very room that you have been occupying for the last few weeks. There are the two Phillips Oppenheims you left behind, half a packet of cigarettes, and four attempts in pencil at a girl's (Jean's?) face, all there to testify to you. The very ham (but not the eggs) I have just had for breakfast must have been bought for you and not for me. And now you are in London. I know that, not because I have received any of the explanatory letters and telegrams that you must have sent careering round the country, but because Trump here told me last night.

You see what happened? I got your letter about Marjorie, which had been delayed several days, by the second post the day before yesterday. I immediately settled things at Peartree Lodge, and left for Keswick early yesterday morning, sending a telegram, of course. I went roaring through England – with the rain lashing against the carriage windows – all yesterday, entertaining myself at times with imaginary conversations with Marjorie and you. It was already dark when I landed in Keswick. I was disappointed not to find you at the station, but as it was a foul night, wetter than ever, with great gusts of wind blowing through the cracks in the hills, I could hardly blame you for not being there. If I was the sensible man I pretend to be, I should have stayed in Keswick last night. But the daft old maggot of adventure had got into my brain, and I was determined to push on to the Brown Bull. Four taximen refused to entertain the idea of going out to Garrowdale, but the fifth – one of those youngsters who always have cigarettes in the corners of their mouths and look absolutely useless, but who would cheerfully drive a car up to the gates of Hell – positively jumped with joy at the idea. I sat in front with him (it was the least I could do), and together we went through a little black wet Odyssey. You know what it is like driving out to Garrowdale in broad daylight, so perhaps you can imagine what a journey we had last night through the wind and rain. It took two hours, with intervals – for magneto trouble – between the acts. The hero of the piece (his name is George Shepherd) never turned a hair. His favourite phrase is 'You know what it is!' and the worse things were the more cheerfully he brought it out. I have decided that I would rather write a book about George Shepherd and 'You know what it is' than about the Chimera of Romanticism.

You can imagine the rest, the triumphant arrival at the Brown Bull, the instant inquiry for you, the devastating news that you had rushed off to London that very morning. Trump, who had obviously spent a dull day and was thinking of going to bed when we arrived, enjoyed himself immensely, pointing out how you and I had missed one another.

'You're a thoughtful man, sir, I can see that,' he said, after he had seen to some supper for us. 'You won't be surprised at a thing like this. It's typical, that's what it is, typical. All hurry, hurry, hurry. And where are we going? We don't know. Nobody knows. It's all become like a kally-aid-ascope. No plan, you see, sir. What we want is an *aristo*cracy of the intellect. If Man can't control his own destiny, who's going to do it for him? that's the question.'

'Trump.' A gigantic female voice came from somewhere behind the bar.

'Just a minute,' he said to us, in quite a different tone, 'that's the wife calling.' And away he scurried.

George Shepherd gave me a wink. 'He can talk the hind-leg off a donkey,' he remarked, 'but he doesn't wear the trousers here. Nice little feller, though, and it's a good billet here. You'll be all right here.' Very soon he was mounting his car again, to return through that roaring wet darkness to Keswick. I had suggested he should stay the night at the Brown Bull, but he wouldn't hear of it. Even then I had to give him more than he asked for, though he was sensible enough to take it. I went out to see him off.

'Hope you have a better journey back,' I said to him. 'I'm afraid I've let you in for something to-night.'

'That's nothing. All in the game,' he replied. 'You know what it is.' A roar of the engine, and he was gone.

When I went back and Trump began to tell me what the world wanted, I said that what it really needed was more Shepherdism. But I couldn't make him understand. I was very tired then, and after refusing the loan of Winwood Reade's *Martyrdom of Man*, which Trump pressed upon me, I went off to bed and soon fell asleep.

Now breakfast has come and gone and I am smoking my second pipe. It is still raining hard, and as I stare out of the window (catching just a glimpse of your Farthing Hall), the Garrowdale I praised to you seems an old idle dream.

Later.

I left this letter open and went off to have a yarn with Trump (who would be a very sensible chap if he had never read anything), thinking that something might happen later in the day. It has done. After lunch it cleared up, so I went for a short walk just to sniff the mountain air and have a look at Farthing Hall. I am, of course, thinking a great deal more about Marjorie and my own affairs than about yours, but I haven't yet thought of what I should do about going over to Lambdale. Off I went then, past Farthing Hall, which looked very grey, sullen and desolate, and up the lonely twisting road that you must know so well now. I did not meet a soul until I had turned round and was about three-quarters of a mile from the Brown Bull. Then I saw someone coming my way. It was a girl with two dogs. When we were closer, I saw that it was quite a young girl, dark, pale slim. I could see her face quite well when she drew near, because she was not wearing a hat. This could only be your Jean Rossett. I had about ten seconds in which to make up my mind what to do. I knew that any hesitation would be fatal, so I walked straight up and planted myself in front of her.

'Pardon me, but are you Miss Rossett?' I asked. She obviously was, and without giving her time to say anything, I went on: 'I came here to find my friend, Mark French. He has gone back to London, apparently, and I am wondering if possibly you have any message from him for me. My name is Newlands.'

When I had first addressed her, she had looked panic-stricken, probably because she imagined that I was a money-lender or a detective looking for her brother. Then when I mentioned you, at once she looked relieved and embarrassed.

'Yes, I've heard' – here she hesitated a moment – 'Mr French mention you as his greatest friend. I'm so sorry you've missed him. You see, I'm – I'm afraid it's my fault, because I asked him to go.'

Then, when I murmured something about it not mattering, she did a fine thing. With one brave sweep, she cleared away all shyness, embarrassment, doubts, hesitations, possible suspicions, lifted her chin and fastened eyes that were honest and yet haunted upon my face.

'Mr Newlands,' she began. 'I'm sure Mr French——' She hesitated. 'I'm sure he has told you something of what has been happening here. He has gone to try and help my brother. Perhaps I ought to have gone myself, but I felt I couldn't leave my father, who hasn't been very well lately.'

'Mark will do everything possible,' I said quickly. 'You may be sure of that.'

'Yes, I know. Though I ought not to have sent him. I had no right.'

'Don't worry about that. You must know that you had every right.'

She was looking very troubled now. 'There was no one else,' she said moodily. 'I thought and thought about it.'

'You couldn't have prevented him from helping you,' I told her. 'I can assure you that Mark will have no peace until he has done everything possible to help you out of all your difficulties.'

'He should never have come here,' she burst out. 'It was hard enough before he came, but it was worse afterwards. But I wanted – oh, I don't know! – someone who might understand – just a few moments of life all my own – something to think about. But I see now that that was wrong, that I ought to have refused to speak to him at first, that he ought never to have come.'

'Would you really have been happier if he had never come at all?' I asked, looking her in the eyes. It was a cruel question, but I felt that it would be easier afterwards if she was compelled to say what she really felt about you.

'Yes,' she answered quickly and falsely, just as we answer all day long. Then she brought up the truth, as I knew she would. 'No, I wouldn't really. Deep down I'm glad. It makes everything different, and I shan't ever forget.'

It doesn't matter what I replied to that. There is only one person who could have replied to it properly, and that is the particular chuckle-headed complacent male whose image she takes with her on these walks, in short, your entirely undeserving self. We walked some way together and talked about you. I told her a little of my own ridiculous history, which left her outwardly demure but, I fancy, quite amused and excited inside. In fact, I think, it did her good; she's heard about no troubles but those of her wretched family for some time, so that a glimpse of my serio-comic worries did her no harm at all. From all this you will gather that we became friends almost at once.

When we finally returned to within fifty yards or so of Farthing Hall, she stopped and put a hand on my arm. Something very serious was coming, I could see that. 'Listen, Mr Newlands,' she began, very earnestly. 'If you want to help me – and perhaps Mark too – there is something you can do. Will you please come and meet my father as soon as it's possible, and spend as much time with him as you can? He's hasty and rather eccentric, but he's a gentleman, however queer he may be sometimes, and I'm sure you would find him very interesting. I know, too, that he'd love talking to you. Mark is too young——'

'But I'm old enough for anything, a contemporary of his, is that it?'

She could laugh now. 'No, I'm sorry, I didn't mean that. But you must know what I meant. You will come, won't you? Perhaps to-morrow. I'll try to arrange something.'

We left it at that. I like her enormously, Mark, more than any girl I've met these past two years. Go in and win. All your rhapsodies and knight-errantry are not out of place with her, for she's that kind of girl. Talking to her after the London minxes is like walking out of surf and wreckage into the sunshine of Prospero's island: she is one of the Mirandas. And now I am wondering what to do about meeting that Rosalind of mine.

Yours ever,
ROBERT.

20 JERMYN STREET.

MY DEAR BOB,

Half an hour ago I found your long and most interesting letter at the club. I have only five minutes now, but I am scribbling this in order to tell you how your meeting with Jean has thrilled me. I am putting your letter in my pocket and shall look at it several times during the evening; you have brought her so close to me that I feel that she is here with me in the room now. And I can't tell you what your liking her means to me; you're the best friend I have in the world, and I value your opinion about people and things a great deal more than it's good for you to know. You've made me almost dizzy with excitement; there's a kind of grand reassurance to me in your letter, as though I knew now that this thing were really going to come off for me. You see, although I couldn't but feel during the last week up there that I was beginning to mean something to her I hadn't any real assurance of it. It isn't that one's too modest, God knows, but rather that when you want anything terribly badly you feel that your luck must be out about it; the apple that you long for most never drops into your hand. But that you should admire her and feel while you were talking to her that she was thinking of me, those are two simply marvellous things.

Yes, it's damned funny that you should be up there with Trump just as I'm down here with the ghastly shadow of Jean's brother. You'll find Marjorie in a day or two, I suppose, have a little talk, wonder how you could both have been so foolish, and it will all be over. Then I shall be seeing you both soon again; in fact, so brave is my optimism to-night that I can even fancy that in a few weeks Jean and I and you and Marjorie will all be having a cozy dinner together somewhere. God! don't I wish it were true. But these rooms that I am in don't, I must confess, reassure me. Before your letter came I was loathing them; they have the most sinister, murderous air. I was reading an article somewhere to-day describing one of those little hotels where people go and stay in London, one of those dreadful places where old ladies whisper together and the body is hidden under the sofa. Well, these rooms are like that. No more now, and write here. I will send something off to you soon again. To tell you the truth, it cheers me up to put 'The Brown Bull' on the envelope. How I love that valley with its wind and rain and quiet!

Yours ever,
MARK.

20 JERMYN STREET.
MY DEAR BOB,

I am following my last night's letter with another, not because anything
has happened, but the fact is that the knowledge of your being five
minutes away from Jean and perhaps at this very moment seeing her
makes me so restless that I am having all that I can do to hold myself
down and not to rush up to you both by the very next train. But I won't
go until I've got on to that miserable lad young Rossett, who is skulking
somewhere. To-night I intend to penetrate into the secrets of that low
haunt of his; I have found out where it is, and I shall spend a miserable
evening there, I suppose. I loathe night clubs and all their citizens, and
this must be, from what I hear, one of the very worst. To-day there is
frost, and London is both shadowless and silent; there is an opalescent
bloom on everything, as though Renoir had touched it up; all the
women have a colour like those pink-and-green apples that Renoir was
always painting, and when I walked down Piccadilly just now everybody
seemed to have their fingers on their lips as though they were expecting
at any moment an astonishing outburst of something or other. I was
dining with an American last night, who said that London was too
shabby for anything, and so she is just now, like an old lady muffled up in
a rather dirty grey shawl. But very arrogant, greatly pleased with herself,
telling everybody else to go to hell. As I told the American last night, her
personality is so strong that no foreign influences can do anything with
her at all, and thank God, say I, for it.

But that isn't really what I am thinking of this four o'clock of a
shadowy afternoon in this dreary room where all the furniture stinks of
bachelors who have committed suicide from ennui and loneliness, where
little gusts blow about the room laden with stale whisky, unpaid bills, and
the shabby shufflings of incompetent menservants. And all the time the
elder Rossett's shadow is hanging over me. Strange how the personality
of that probably quite ordinary drunken waster remains with one. It is
partly because he is at present so incomprehensible. Why should he love
me like a long-lost brother, insist on my company, and then suddenly try
to murder me? He says that I was interfering with his family, but I don't
think he cares enough for his family to bother about anyone's
interference, and anyway I was involved so slightly. I am sure that he
knows that I kissed his daughter, and of course I told him that I refused

to lend money to his son, but I fancy that there's something deeper than this in the whole affair. The key to him lies somewhere, I am sure, in his love for the ground that he is standing on, a sort of hysterical superstitious love, I imagine. I can see myself getting a little like that up there; if one stayed long enough quietly in that valley every twig and every bend of the hill might become personal. The contact would make you arrogant, you'd feel that you shared some secret with the place that had been committed only to yourself, you'd resent everyone else as an intruder, you'd get a kind of conceited sense of immortality from it. There's a picture by Utrillo, one of the early better ones, a Paris street, of course, with those white buildings that he's so fond of, and every house in it, every door and every lamp-post has just this sense of self-confident arrogance as though they were all, the windows and the doors and the white walls, whispering to you confidentially, 'You stick to us and together we'll tell the world; you're the one we've been looking for.' I fancy that Rossett has been developing that kind of arrogance, growing so intimate with his three crinkly hills and his chattering river and his long silent road that leads to nowhere that an intruder insults his pride. I don't know and I don't really care, but I want to get back, and I must get back. I'll find the young wastrel, catch him round his dirty neck, haul him back to his father, then take Jean away. Meanwhile, as often as you can let me know that you've seen her I'll be grateful.

Yours ever,
MARK.

THE BROWN BULL.

MY DEAR MARK,

I have just received the second of your two notes. It will, I see, be an act of friendship and Christian charity to tell you everything that happens here, so here goes.

The excitement began yesterday morning, some time between ten and eleven. It was raining hard and so Trump and I were smoking an idle pipe together in the front room, the bar-parlour place, here. It happened that we were both standing at the window, looking out on the grey slant of rain. We heard the sound of an approaching car and, like the idle rustics we are, immediately glued our noses to the pane. A moment later there roared past an enormous saloon car, piled high with luggage; and it was going down the dale, probably to Keswick.

'That's Mrs Masham's car,' said Trump. 'It looks as if she's clearing off or else taking her friends down to the station.' And then he wanted to talk about the Masham, but I cut him short, saying that I knew her. I wanted to think for a minute. Was Marjorie in that car? Had they all gone? And if Marjorie was in that car tearing down to Keswick station to catch the first train to Lord-knows-where, what the devil was I to do, stuck there like a fool? You can imagine what I felt. It seemed to be raining twice as hard, and suddenly I came to the conclusion that poor little Trump was a dreadful bore.

I began to question him. Could I telephone to Lambdale? No, I couldn't. Could I send a message there? No, I couldn't do that, except on Wednesdays and Saturdays, when a carrier went up there. I could use the post, of course, but that would take at least two days.

'I wonder if the car's coming back this way,' I said. 'If so, I might stop it.'

'Well, you never know, you never know,' Trump replied. 'It's like everything else; you never know. If they've just gone to the station, it'll come back this way; but they might have gone away in it. You see, it's all rush and scurry now with these people – here to-day and gone to-morrow. Besides, if it does come back, it might be gone past before you can stop it. That's how it is, you see.'

I did see, and went up to my room, partly because I thought of writing a note and partly because I wanted to get away from Trump's maddening philosophising. I stared out at the rain and the misty tops and wondered if I could possibly walk over to Lambdale. I was in an absurd position, particularly as I didn't want to take Trump into my confidence. I felt at once baffled and depressed.

Then I heard voices below, went out on to the landing, and discovered that the visitor was Jean. I went down and found her just concluding some business – about eggs – with Mrs Trump. She smiled at me, rather shyly, out of those pretty dark eyes of hers, and I took her on one side at once and told her what had happened. 'You see,' I concluded, 'I don't even know if she's there or not now.'

'How dreadful for you!' she cried, and thought for a moment. 'I think the car was only going to the station, because that's the time it usually passes. And the chauffeur nearly always calls here on the way back. I believe Mrs Trump has some signal to make him stop because she often sends things – eggs and chickens and other things – to Lambdale. I'll ask her.' And off she went.

She returned in a minute to say that the car would be stopped on its way back – to my great relief. We then talked about you, and she said too that she had not heard anything about her brother and was feeling terribly worried. Then she told me that her father, who was feeling very bored and lonely, had pricked up his ears when she had casually remarked that there was a visitor, an Oxford don or an author or something, staying at the inn.

'He'll be coming across,' she went on, smiling a little, 'pretending to see Mr Trump about something, but really hoping to have a look at you. I know you're dreadfully worried about your own affairs——'

'I don't know that I'm dreadfully worried,' I said hastily, 'but of course a man wants to settle a matter of this kind——'

'Of course you're dreadfully worried,' she told me, coolly. 'You want to make it up, don't you? You're missing Mrs Newlands like anything, I know you are.' And then she suddenly felt she was saying too much, and faltered: 'I'm sorry – I – I shouldn't have said that, should I? Are you annoyed?'

'Not a bit,' I told her.

'About father, though – you will make friends with him, won't you, as you promised? I haven't said anything to him about your being a friend of Mark's, and I thought perhaps it would be better if you didn't say anything. Do you mind?' And then when I said that I didn't, she went on hastily: 'That's cowardly and deceitful, isn't it – not telling him anything? But he'll only lose his temper and perhaps quarrel with you – and – and I do want him to keep from worrying just now. Talking to someone like you would do him such a lot of good. When he stays at home, seeing nobody new, and he's in one of these moods, he's just like a bomb, and we creep about thinking he'll go off at any moment.' Then she laughed, then she looked grave, then she gave me a friendly smile, and it did my heart good to see her.

We talked a little longer, and then she ran away and left me to wait for the car. I was just sitting down to lunch when I heard it coming up the road. Mrs Trump's signal — which I discovered to be a petrol tin placed nearly in the middle of the road — succeeded in pulling up the car. I hurried out and found there was no one in the car but the chauffeur, who walked back with me into the inn. I told him I was acquainted with Mrs Masham, and asked him if she had left home. But no, it appeared that she was still there; he had only been taking some visitors to the station.

This left me rather breathless. 'Hadn't you a Mrs Newlands staying with you?' I asked as casually as I could contrive. 'I suppose she's just gone too.'

'Mrs Newlands is the only one that hasn't gone, sir,' said he — bless him! — 'she's staying on for some time.'

It was all right then. You can imagine my relief. 'Wait here a minute and ask Trump to give you a drink, and I will write a little note to Mrs Newlands.' And it was a little note too. I simply wrote:

MY DEAR MARJORIE,

I am staying at the Brown Bull, Garrowdale. When and where can I see you? I had hoped to find Mark here, but he has gone back to London.

But when I had given it to the chauffeur and seen the car vanish into the rain, I felt that something had been accomplished, something done, and returned to the fire in the bar-parlour place to smoke the kind of pipe one achieves after turning a corner in a difficult chapter. I had had a wild impulse to climb into the car myself and see her that very afternoon, but I saw that that would be a bad move. I spent a pleasant half-hour trying to imagine Marjorie's face when she received my note, and wondering how soon she would reply and what she would say. After so much Mashamism, I thought, she would find even me a welcome companion.

In the middle of the afternoon, I heard a voice booming after Trump outside in the hall. This, I thought, must be the great Rossett. And so it was. He came in and introduced himself, with a voice like a foghorn and a fist like a leg of mutton; he reminds me of some High-Church-and-Tory squire of the early eighteenth century. Well, he was a Rossett, he said, and they'd been in Garrowdale a few hundred years.

'There were some Rossetts of Garrowdale mixed up in the '15 and the '45,' I remarked. 'Is it the same family?'

You should have seen him light up at that. He glowed and roared in triumph and approbation. 'The very same, the very same. Hamilton

Rossett escaped from Carlisle, came to these fells, where they couldn't find him, sir, couldn't get a sight of him. And I could do the same to-day, for all their motor cars and wireless messages; I could outwit a couple of regiments in these fells. And so you've heard of Hamilton Rossett and his two lads. Come over to my house, sir, and I'll show you their portraits and you shall have the whole story. It's a pleasure, sir, to meet a man nowadays who knows the history of his country. Oxford, didn't you say?'

I hadn't said, but did now, gave him my college, and promptly received the information that he had gone up to Merton in Eighty-Four, and had been sent down in the middle of his second year merely 'for keeping a damned interfering old parson locked in his room.' But he bore the place no malice, he added; after all, it was the only place left where a gentleman might decently go to be educated. We exchanged a few remarks about Oxford and then he pressed me to dine with him that night. 'Haven't talked to a soul for weeks except a young pup of a painter' – meaning you, my dear Mark – 'and so I'll take no denial. I can give you a decent glass of wine, and there aren't many left.'

So I went. That was last night. Jean was there – quiet, rather ghostly, but every now and then flashing a signal of relief and gratitude from her dark eyes – and the nondescript elderly female, who never uttered one word. They both left us after dinner and I never saw them again. Rossett produced some extraordinarily good port and some really fine brandy, and before I left had filled himself with liquor and glory. I can't describe the evening because there isn't time. The postman will be here any moment to take away the morning post and I am scribbling away so furiously that I am beginning to wonder if you will ever be able to read this.

No news yet from Marjorie, but I could hardly expect any. The postman's below; I must close this now.

Yours,
ROBERT.

P.S. – There's a car here too. It's Mrs Masham's. Nobody in it but the chauffeur. He must have a message. I'll let you know everything as soon as I can.

MY DEAR BOB,

Your letter just received. It has rather bewildered me; I see you standing in the door of the Brown Bull watching motor cars whizzing past, wondering whether Marjorie is in this one or that one, and finally, rather remarkably, doing nothing about it. I feel millions of miles away; you have reduced by your mere presence the whole Rossett family to more ordinary terms – Jean is a pretty girl with dark eyes, the elder Rossett a good old country squire, Farthing Hall itself an ordinary little country house. I can see that in your own mind you have found me absurdly unreal with my whole view of that romantic scene; it isn't romantic to you at all, and I'm a silly young ass in love with an ordinary girl who has got a drunken old tyrant of a father, a sweep of a brother, and is otherwise in no way different from a million other English girls.

Still I keep my vision. There is something dangerous and terrifying in life and one is for ever almost treading on its tail – almost, mind you, but never quite. If my adventures have any meaning at all it is that I have discovered beauty and terror in my love for Jean and my consciousness of old Rossett's almost mad sense of the land he is living on. It is as though his feet were rooted in the ground and he insists that everything round him must be rooted there too; and here I come, a stranger from nowhere, and try to detach both his son and his daughter. He stamps on the ground with meaningless rage and all the hills re-echo approvingly. I shall watch your prosaic interpretation of him with deep admiration for your skilful seeing of things as they are; I never should; that's why we're friends, I suppose.

Meanwhile I've met and talked to the whelp. I saw some very unpleasant human beings last night. The 'Dolphin' is so little ashamed of itself that its address is in the telephone book; I found my way there in a taxi, a little dark street off Russell Square. I pushed back a door, stumbled up a wooden crooked staircase, opened another door, and fell straight into the arms of a little man with a lisp and a toupet who was sitting behind a large visitors' book and staring into vacancy. I never saw anyone more alone. In the room beyond him there didn't seem to be a soul, there wasn't a sound anywhere. Himself he might have been a Tussaud waxwork, one of those figures in the old, now, alas! devastated, Chamber of Horrors, Crippen or Seddon or the bath man, frozen yellow and polite in a wooden suit of evening clothes. I said that I was a friend of Mr Rossett's and he let me in without a murmur. After that I sat behind a little table in the dreariest looking room imaginable; the floor was cleared for dancing, the walls were covered with lively paintings – nude persons with green posteriors and purple faces. Not a soul to be seen. After a while the gaunt shambling waiter sidled up to me as though he were going to confide in my ear some loathsome secret and asked me what I'd drink. I ordered something, and then he murmured to me in a voice of desperate melancholy that it was a little early, the ladies and gentlemen had not arrived yet. They didn't arrive for another three-quarters of an hour, and I sat there remembering all my sins, counting up all my unkindnesses, my malevolences and my stupidities, growing chillier and chillier, wishing even for a traitorous moment that I had never seen Cumberland or any of the Rossetts; even the thought of Jean was no use to me. In another five minutes I should have cut my throat; not that it would have caused any sensation if I had, the lanky waiter would have swept me up and the little man with the toupet buried me under the coat-rack. But my life was saved by the noisy appearance of a number of young gentlemen and ladies. Oh Bob! but they were a ratty-looking lot. When I think of the gay descriptions that I have encountered in the works of Mr Michael Arlen and others of London's night-club life and think of that miserable bunch, the young women masquerading as boys, the men uneasy and gloomy as though they expected to be haled off to penal servitude at any moment, the wretched little band – two coloured men and a girl with orange hair – the dreary treadmill kind of gestures with which they paced the floor, the chilly air and a strange sort of hushed atmosphere as though everyone had been ordered to speak in a whisper.

After a little while a girl came over and talked to me. She must have been very young. She was so thin that the wind seemed to whistle through her, and so tired that she could scarcely keep her eyes open. She asked me to dance with her and I did, if you can call it dancing. We wandered round the room and all her sharp bones dug into my body like knives. We sat down afterwards at my little table; I gave her a drink, and she then asked me to marry her. She wasn't drunk, she was only infinitely weary and depressed. She told me that she liked the look of me and that if I married her (that is, if I wasn't married already) I could live with her for a month or two and she would then have no sore feelings at my departure. She said that she was herself a good sort and could be very bright and amusing when she had had a little sleep. She thought it was time she was married again, she'd got to find someone, and she didn't trust any of the men she knew. I asked her whether it wouldn't be better if we should see a little of one another first, and she answered me very seriously that that was just the trouble, if you saw a fellow for a week or two you'd be certain not to marry him, the only thing to do was to take someone on the chance. I said that for all she knew I might be the most desperate sort of criminal, be arrested to-morrow for forging cheques or anything, and what would she do then? She replied that I couldn't be worse than the men she knew and I looked a good deal better, and that she had a friend who had just drawn a man's name out of a hat and married him the next day and it had turned out very well. I told her then that I couldn't marry her because I was in love with somebody else, but she said that that didn't matter in the least, I could be in love with as many girls as I pleased; it was time she was married again, and a complete stranger was the only hope. I rather liked her; we were getting along very well indeed, and then suddenly I saw that young Rossett was in the room staring at me. He came over to me at once and was apparently delighted to see me; he put on the friendliest manner he possessed – just about as friendly as a young snake in the Zoo. He had his usual furtive manner, and I could see that such brains as he had were working hard on propitiating me. I needn't tell you that he's got his work cut out to do that. He's frightened, Bob, with more than the ordinary fears; you'd think that he'd got somebody round the corner waiting to hit him on the head with a hammer. Perhaps he has, but the oddest thing was that on this occasion for the first time I saw his relationship with Jean. There was something in his voice, the turn of his head, that reminded me of her; I could almost hear her voice behind him saying, 'He is part of me whether you like it or no.' I told him brusquely enough, while the bony young woman was watching and listening with all her eyes and ears, that I wanted to have a talk with him. I asked him to come and see me and he said eagerly that he would; he was ready to come back with me there and then, but I thought that we should talk better in daylight with plenty of people within hail. He brought up then and introduced to me one of the nastiest men I have ever seen, a large big fleshy man with a white flabby face, a streak of black moustache and a soft soapy voice. When Rossett went off to get some drinks, this gentleman became very confidential, informed me that he was the boy's best friend. He then added that young Rossett had a beautiful sister, that he'd met her several times, and that young Rossett had promised that he should know her a great deal better. He then winked at me and smiled a greasy smile; it was all that I could do not to hit him in his horrible face. As a matter of fact I was extremely kind and cordial. Young Rossett returned and looked at this fat villain, whose name by the way I found to be Mulligan, with a mixture of apprehension, dislike and sycophancy that was very revealing. I shouldn't wonder but that Mr Mulligan is the key to a good deal of the Rossett mystery. However, having made my appointment with young Rossett, I departed. The bony young woman begged to be allowed to accompany me; I was kind but firm. It was amazing to come out into Russell Square, see a sky full of stars, lighted windows, and to hear a woman singing from some room. I am in for a pretty stiff job, I fancy; I will let you know how it goes.

Yours affectionately,
MARK.

THE BROWN BULL.

MY DEAR MARK,

Thanks for your News from the Night Club. I have always suspected it was like that; a lot of poor young devils half asleep, with here and there a fat rascal. If fashionable vice is so dull and unattractive, virtue can afford to go swaggering down the middle of the road; the Devil is no longer the merry gentleman.

I don't know what you mean when you say I am 'rather remarkably, doing nothing about it.' Did I not tell you in my last, that I had had the car stopped and had sent a note to Marjorie? It wasn't necessary for me to do any more or I should have done it. Did I tell you about the answer? No, of course I didn't; I remember now; I had to give the postman my last letter to you while the car was at the door. Well, the chauffeur had brought a note, and as soon as I saw that it was in Marjorie's perky little handwriting, I found myself hurrying inside with it, quite excited. Here it is:

How impetuous of you! Mrs Masham, who remembers your delightful hospitality, wants you to come over and stay here, but I pointed out that it would be embarrassing and even rather improper to have you under this roof altogether. So you are invited to lunch, this very day, and the car will bring you here and take you back again. It will be rather an awkward little lunch party, just the three of us, so do you think you could bring another man with you? What about the man who lives opposite? Do you know him?

Yours,
MARJORIE.

A very cool but prickly little note, you see, and of course tremendously Marjorie-ish. I could hear her mocking voice in it, could see her glance and lifted eyebrows.

I saw at once that it would be better if I could take Rossett along, for then he and the Masham could amuse one another while Marjorie and I talked. (Now wouldn't you have thought that too? Of course you would, and so would any other man. We are too innocent to live — as you shall see.) There was plenty of time. The chauffeur settled down for a gossip with Trump, and I strolled over to Farthing Hall to persuade Rossett to accompany me.

The first person I saw there was Jean. She looked quite startled, and is evidently living in terror of hearing bad news. Her very first words were: 'Have you – had a letter – from Mark?'

'Not since I saw you last,' I told her. 'I shall probably have one to-morrow. Is anything wrong – I mean specially wrong?'

She looked relieved. 'No, only when I saw you – I wondered——' But she didn't say what she wondered.

'I only came to tell your father he had been invited out to lunch with me to-day, by Mrs Masham.'

She lit up at this. 'Why,' she cried, 'he's not been out to lunch for years and years! I simply can't imagine him going out now. Still, he might, you know. I'll go and tell him. He's not up yet.'

Off she went, and in about five minutes Rossett himself came down, in an enormous old dressing-gown full of holes and stained with liquor. 'Hello!' he roared, obviously glad to see me. 'How do you find yourself this morning, sir? Head buzzing?'

'Not a bit. Clear as a bell.'

'That's right. So do I. There isn't a headache or a touch of liver in *my* liquor, I can tell you. I laid it down before they began bottling the sewers, eh, before they began calling in the damned chemists, eh! Well, what's this about lunching?'

I told him, laying stress on the fact that Mrs Masham had specially asked me to bring him. She had, I assured him, a passion for this country.

'And wants to have another look at a Rossett, eh?' he boomed. 'We're part of the country by this time, I should think. Well, I don't know. I'm devilish rusty, haven't left this valley these last few years, and there's nobody here but oafs and fools and rascals, and I can't eat with them. But I see you're set on it, and I'd like to oblige you, even if it means eating French snippets and trying to drink widow's wine from the chemist's. But how are we going to get there?'

When I told him the car was waiting for us and would also bring us back, he could not hide his gratification. I could see that he imagined that the whole affair had been arranged for his benefit and in his honour. He stood there, turning his dingy dressing-gown into the plumes of a swelling turkey-cock.

Half an hour afterwards he came down again, ready for the feast, very spruce indeed in a check suit and a very high collar, and looking like a beau of 1900. Nevertheless, I must admit that he looked a magnificent old ruffian, and I felt that if the Masham was at all impressionable he would catch her eye at once. All the way there he was in great form, and I artfully fed his vanity. You would have thought the very hills themselves were there by his permission, and had been first conjured into the world by his grandfather, old 'Bingo' Rossett, who ran away with Lady Letty

Lanbury. I assure you, my dear Mark, I know more about the Rossett family now than I do about my own. One thing he admitted, though – that financially he is now on his last legs. He is at his wits' end in his attempt to keep the family rooted here, and, obviously, Jean is to be sacrificed in this great cause.

When I saw Marjorie, my heart gave a leap and then a thump or two. Being away from me – confound it! – seems to agree with her, for I never saw her looking better. But she was obviously on her mettle and ready to enjoy the whole thing. She wore that dangerously demure look. Even Rossett was struck, and addressed himself to her and not to the Masham, who wore a kind of turban and looked more ridiculous than ever. That was before we sat down to lunch. The food was quite good, and the wine – an old Chambertin – even better, so that Rossett beamed approval. But it happened that just after we sat down, Mrs Masham made one of her idiotic remarks to Rossett. She said in her gushing way: 'Do you know, Mr Rossett, my friend Mrs Carslake-Pyle swears that there are fairies and pixies here. She's seen them. And I'm sure I did too, last week, not two miles from here, dear little things in red and green. Can't you tell us about them?'

Rossett stared at her in amazement, then burst into a colossal guffaw. 'Fairies! Pixies!' he roared. 'What d'you think this place is, ma'am, a Drury Lane pantomime? We Rossetts have been here for centuries and never heard of such a thing. I know these dales better than most people know the palms of their own hands, but – pixies indeed! – sheep, ma'am! – bits of bracken! – bits of ling! – that's what you saw.'

The poor Masham smiled in a feeble sort of way and immediately afterwards turned to me, to tell me that she had just begun a new work, Solar Harmony or Lunar Discords or something of that kind. I tried to make the conversation general, but it was hopeless. The Masham would not leave me alone, and what was worse – Marjorie and Rossett were hard at it and would not stop. It was, of course, just mischief on her part. After a time I sat silent and the Masham had little to say, but the other two never stopped. Will you believe me when I say that Marjorie and I never exchanged a single remark during the whole lunch? However, I consoled myself – or tried to console myself, for I was beginning to feel dubious – with the thought that Marjorie was only disposing of Rossett and the lunch together, and that as soon as we left the table, she and I would have our talk. But not a bit of it. Coffee came and went, and Marjorie never made a move in my direction. Every time Rossett came to the end of one of his infernally long stories, she encouraged him to begin another. The Masham nodded off, and I raged inwardly, wishing that I had never brought Rossett with me.

At last Rossett suggested that we ought to be going. He had to say something then to Mrs Masham, so I rushed Marjorie into a corner and opened out at once. 'I thought I was here to talk to you, Marjorie,' I cried.

'Yes, we don't seem to have done much talking, do we, Robert?' she replied, very demurely, but all alight with mischief. 'I shall be here for a few more days, so you had better come again – if Mrs Masham will ask you, and I'm sure she will.'

'I'm not coming here again,' I told her hastily. 'We must meet somewhere else and as soon as we can. We must talk it out, you know.'

'Really, Robert, I hardly recognise you, you are becoming so impatient, so restless. I am beginning to think I ought to be introduced to you – all over again.'

'Do you walk here?'

'Sometimes. When it's fine. I shall probably do more walking now that Mrs Masham is to be busy with her new book. Why?' You would have thought she had just met me.

'Couldn't we meet somewhere, between here and Garrowdale?'

'When I go out by myself,' she said, softly and slowly, 'I sometimes sit near the little bridge, where the road crosses the stream nearly at the head of the dale, you know, and there I eat my sandwiches. I shall probably be there the first reasonably fine day, perhaps to-morrow.'

'I'll look for you there,' I said, and turned away.

'But, Robert——'

It sounded so like her old cry to me that I whipped round at once expectantly.

She looked me in the eyes and a tiny smile crept into her face. 'You must bring your own sandwiches,' she said, very softly.

It is, I think, only in novels that people say 'Bah!' or 'Pshaw!' but I suppose the noise I made then would have to be translated into something like that to be set down at all. Five minutes later Rossett and I were in the car. He was still immensely pleased with himself.

'Extraordinarily attractive woman that. Sensible too. What's her name?' he asked. 'Couldn't catch it.'

'Mrs Newlands.' There was no help for it.

'Newlands, eh? That's queer. Any relation?'

'Yes, my wife.'

'Your wife! Well, I'll be damned!' And he burst out into a bellow of laughter, and for two or three minutes rolled and rocked. After that, of course, I had to tell him a little, and he listened with many a stare and a snort, and, I fancy, set me down as a milksop. He didn't say so in so many words, but it was clear that he thought I ought to have given Marjorie a good beating. I wished him far enough, dead drunk in the worst night club in London. Why can't he go himself and look after his beastly son?

That was yesterday. This morning it is drizzling, and I am wondering whether it is worth while trudging those six or seven miles on the off-chance of finding Marjorie at the bridge. I must make up my mind this next quarter of an hour, but in the meantime I get this letter ready for the post, which goes out in about ten minutes. I wish you could see this place now, in the drizzle, and then you might not be so sure I am merely prosaic. I think it must have been all sunshine, moonshine and thunder-and-lightning when you were here. It's the bleakest prose this morning.

Yours,
ROBERT.

20 JERMYN STREET.

MY DEAR BOB,

I may tell you that I am touched and pleased at your writing me such full accounts of your adventures in the North. You're doing it partly, I suppose, because your excitement (and hide it though you may, you are excited) leads you to want an audience, and I am your only possible one, but also because you know how much every minute of the day I am longing for news of that valley. Yes, it's kind of you to bring it so close to me. All the time I am wondering whether Jean won't write me a letter; I watch every post as I haven't since I was a small child at Christmas time. I haven't written to her myself, although I have been aching to do so; I've been afraid it might lead her into trouble with her incredible father. How differently, by the way, he comes out of your view of him; I expect you're right, I've painted him in my own colours, but as a matter of truth there's common ground between our views. He will rather like you, I fancy; he detested me, and is of so impetuous a temperament that, feeling exasperated by me, he just wanted to fling me to hell. With him, I should imagine, feeling is always translated instantly into action; lucky devil! I wish I were made that way.

Well, now, isn't London the most extraordinary place! Have you ever noticed when you've been here how certain faces and figures keep cropping up in the crowds and theatres and shops. It may be somebody with whom you have a very slight acquaintance, or it may be somebody whom you don't know at all, but like themes in poetry or music again and again they appear, until at last you really begin to feel that you must have some kind of secret connection with them. In the old days when I was going to the Slade (God forgive me for those misspent and wasted hours) there used to be a little old woman in a black bonnet with bugles and shabby shoes that flapped on the pavement. I saw her a hundred times always hurrying somewhere, never looking at me, but all the same I felt that she and I would one day be connected with one another; I should bang her on the head for her hoarded treasure or elope with her beautiful daughter. But I was wrong, you see, she never appears any more now, and yet I know her so much more intimately than I do most of my friends. In the same way I have seen the fat white-faced slug of a man whom I met at the night club the other evening three separate times, and on the last I had some words with him. I think he haunts the streets and

pubs round Leicester Square; once I have seen him in Charing Cross
Road, once waiting outside the Alhambra, and yesterday afternoon I
followed him into a bar on the other side of Anthony Young's the
hairdresser, two doors from the Prince of Wales's Theatre. In Charing
Cross Road I followed a little way behind him, and one thing I noticed
about him at once was that no female, young or old, plain or lovely,
passed him without receiving his full attention. He is one of those men –
and I believe there are a great many of them in the world – to whom
women are a constant, unceasing, thrilling and despairing preoccupation.
I knew a man like this once; women were never out of his mind, he was
for ever hoping to get something from them that would satisfy his thirst,
though of course he never did. He shot himself later. I don't think that
this fat-faced friend of young Rossett's will ever shoot himself, he hasn't
the pluck, but there is something terribly tragic and unspeakably
disgusting in the glance that he gives a woman, so eager, so inquisitive, so
furtive, so apprehensive, so bold, so hungry and so sterile. Well, to cut
this short, I followed him yesterday into a little pub like a mouse-trap
near the Prince of Wales's Theatre. He ordered a drink at the bar as
though he were an old habitué of the place. He was rather magnificently
and yet rather shabbily dressed; he had a large sham pearl in his tie, faded
spats on his shoes and rings on his fingers. He talked to two cronies but
never took his eyes for a moment off the barmaid, a plain enough girl,
who obviously knew him well. His mind was on his talk with his friends
but his appetites were absorbed by the barmaid; two detached parts of
him moving in different directions. Not that he had any hope of her, he
had probably attacked her long ago and been well smacked for his pains,
but she was a woman and therefore a symbol.

After a while, he turned round and saw me standing at his elbow. He
didn't remember me in the least. He would talk, I suppose, to any
stranger with the thought that in some way or another there might be
something to be got out of him, and all the time he looked at the
barmaid with that unhappy, restless, greedy gaze, and you can imagine,
Bob, what my feelings were when I reflected that once he had looked at
Jean in that same damned way, and it wouldn't be her young brother's
fault if he didn't look at her soon again. I made a resolve there and then
in that lousy, greasy pub, that I wouldn't leave young Rossett and his
friend alone until I had finished their part in this history once and for all.
I swore a solemn oath to myself standing there, following my fat friend's
dazed appraisal of the barmaid's peroxide shingle. Our talk didn't amount
to much, but it had just this in it; he asked me where I came from
(speaking as it were through the ribs of the barmaid). I said Cumberland,
looking him straight in the eye. Oh yes, he said in his horribly pleasant
and poisonous manner, as though, while he complimented you on your

health, his hand was in your pocket feeling for your watch, he had some friends in Cumberland, one particular friend. Some damn fine girls in Cumberland, he added, his misted eye rolling straight into the mouth of the barmaid, there was a girl in Cumberland he knew — but there I interrupted him, I couldn't bear it for another moment. I, the most dilatory of mortals, would have taken him by the throat and shaken his beastly eyes out of his loathsome face. I turned abruptly on my heel, paid for my drink and left. And to-morrow young Rossett comes to see me. How clean and sweet your valley sounds, how live and real your Marjorie! What I would give for your own true company! Dear Bob, I feel as though I were moving in a dark and dirty country. I love you very much; I hope you'll write as often as you can.

Yours affectionately,
MARK.

                                                            THE BROWN BULL.
MY DEAR MARK,

You seem to me to be having a horrible time. But what exactly are you
doing – I mean, besides peeping into dirty little saloon bars and
meditating on the strange creatures that come up now and then from
London's deep? You are rapidly becoming like one of those Dickens
characters, the mysterious ones that have something to do with the plot
and keep popping up and making enigmatical remarks. Probably you feel
that you are in the same atmosphere that Dickens knew – that of London
turned sinister, the dark city that a lost child might see.

This, I'm afraid, will be rather a muddled letter. I felt cold and shivery
yesterday morning, suspected a chill, and so have taken large doses of
ammoniated tincture of quinine. I don't know how this stuff affects you
(probably you don't take it yet – it's part of the compromise one makes
with the world), but it always leaves me very muzzy in the head. I want
to tell you all that's happening here, but you must not expect a neat
ordered narrative.

We're sort of turning ourselves into a string quartet here: Marjorie first
violin, high and sure and mocking; Self second violin, following on as
best I can; the Masham the viola, wondering and plaintive; Rossett the
rumbling 'cello. What's Jean then? – l hear you ask. She's not really in this
at all; but if you insist on turning her into an instrument too, then she's
the lonely clarionet. (Do you know that lovely quintet of Brahms?) – You
know the way the four instruments chime together, then separate, come
together again, run away, form little alliances, break them, and so on and
so forth? Well, we shall be like that soon.

I can't remember where I left off in my last letter. Wasn't it when I was
wondering if I could venture out in the rain to see Marjorie at the little
bridge near the head of Lambdale? Anyhow, I didn't go because the
drizzle soon became a downpour and I knew Marjorie wouldn't be there.
I stayed here and had a long argument with Trump about Shakespeare.
Trump brought in his ridiculous little cherrywood pipe to see me, and
began talking about Shakespeare, giving me the astounding news that all
Shakespeare's chief characters represent some virtue or vice (Othello is
Jealousy, and so forth). People like Trump are so wrong that as a rule I
don't even bother to contradict them, don't even know where to begin
to set them right. This time I did bother and did know, and lectured

poor Trump solidly and severely for at least an hour. I say 'poor Trump' because at the end of it I suddenly felt sorry for him, but I need not have done, for he was delighted and begged to shake me by the hand. 'I'm not sure that I agree with you, sir,' he proclaimed, 'but I thank you, I thank you. It's food for thought, all that, it is indeed.' It still rained in the afternoon. I didn't want to see Rossett, and was glad that he didn't want to see me. I read some stupid novel, and then dozed off. I was awakened by Mrs Trump, who told me I had a visitor. I rushed down, expecting to see either Rossett or Marjorie, but judge of my surprise when I found it was neither, but Mrs Masham.

Marjorie, though, had come over with her in the car, but had dropped in at Farthing Hall, ostensibly to see some eighteenth-century miniatures that Rossett had promised to show her, but really to make the acquaintance of Jean. 'And I thought I would come in to see you, Mr Newlands, if you don't mind,' the Masham added, rather plaintively for her. She was obviously frightened of Rossett, and, I suspected, was prepared to have a heart-to-heart talk with me about my relations with Marjorie. While I gave her some tea, she continually worked round to the subject of Marjorie, but though I no longer felt any detestation of the woman (who is just fat and silly and, in spite of the ridiculous adulation she sometimes receives, really rather lonely), I had not the slightest desire to discuss Marjorie with her, as you can imagine. So I decided to discuss Rossett instead.

'A very unpleasing type!' the Masham cried. 'I'm sorry if he's really a friend of yours, though I can't believe he is, for I know you're too sensitive, or at least Marjorie has told me, not that I haven't seen it for myself, Mr Newlands. I do not like Mr Rossett. I'm sure he's a man who lives on the lowest possible plane, disgustingly earth-bound. I read it in his glance, at once. If I settle here, as I may, you know, I can only regard him as a drawback. Indeed, I've been wondering if I could buy him out.'

'I'm sure you couldn't do that,' I told her. 'His family has been here for centuries, and he loves every inch of this soil.'

'Earth-bound, as I said,' she put in.

'No, you misjudge him,' I said, determined to accept a brief for Rossett, if only to pass the time. 'Don't you see, his love for his own country, his own land, is rather a fine thing. *You* ought to understand that. He's a very interesting character, and represents a type that is fast disappearing——'

'And a very good thing too. I'm sorry to interrupt, but I'm sure I'm right. I've heard stories about him too. Then I can see for myself. He's Martian, distinctly Martian, and is destined always to sow seeds of discord, war and low sensualities, as the Martians always are.'

'I think you are wrong there,' I told her, wondering where she got this planetary stuff. 'He may appear Martian at first sight, but he's not. He belongs to Jupiter, the proud and commanding. I admit his pride. But think of the long history of his race. Then consider his misfortunes. Remember that he has nobody now, except his daughter, a mere young girl, to confide in, to lean upon in moments of weakness, nobody to soften his pride, to – shall I say? – elevate him. It was only his pride that made him appear so contemptuous when you asked him about the fairies and pixies.'

'Ah! I was coming to that. That was very rude, I thought, besides being a dark denial and proof of spiritual density.' She brought these daft phrases out with an air of mingled triumph and profundity.

'Well, he was so hasty because he hated to think that anybody had seen anything here, in this, his own country, that he hadn't seen. You can understand that, can't you?'

Yes, she could understand that, and I could see she rather liked the look of it. Any scruples I may have had went whistling down the wind; I would be the complete advocate. 'Moreover,' I added softly, 'I may tell you, Mrs Masham, that although he's obviously not a man who makes friends easily, he was – if you will allow me to say so – immensely interested in you and attracted by your personality the other day. Yes, I know what you are going to say. You are going to say that he gave no signs of interest?'

'I was,' replied the Masham, quite grimly for her.

'Pride again!' I cried. 'Pride, you see, and' – and here I lowered my voice – 'a kind of shyness in him. You must not forget that he and I came back here together afterwards, and talked, of course. I say no more than that.'

I did, though. I said a great deal more, but I won't bore you with it. I began this nonsense about Rossett, as I remarked at first, merely to protect myself against any talk of Marjorie or, failing that, any account of Solar Harmony or Lunar Discord or whatever it is she is trying to embalm in another volume. But long before I had done, I was thoroughly enjoying myself.

Then Marjorie hurried in, and the Masham, with elephantine tact, immediately fled in search of the Trumps. Marjorie wasted no time. 'I've been talking to that girl, Robert,' she began, 'that girl of Mark's. He is in love with her, isn't he?'

'Very much. No doubt about that. We don't, of course, know how long——'

She cut me short with one of her lightning gestures. 'Never mind about that,' she said. 'You can keep *that*, Robert, for the time when we discuss *our* affairs. I am talking about these two children now. She is in love with him. And the poor child – she's young even for her age – is in despair. I've told her to go.'

'What!' I stared at her.

'I've told her to go, to run away to Mark, to leave her father – that silly old egoist – and stop worrying about her brother, and to go. Those two worthless men – for the brother's apparently a young scamp – will just squeeze the life out of her if she doesn't. And if she doesn't go soon, she never will. I know. She talks about promises to her mother! No promises ought to keep her at the beck and call of those two men. Her courage is high now, and this is the time. You know, Robert, that I'm not talking about something I don't understand. You know what my life has been or might have been if I hadn't cut the cord. Persuade her, help her, and tell Mark at once what I say. If you don't help this girl, I'll never speak to you again.'

As if I had been refusing for years to lift a finger to help the girl! And Marjorie had only just met her! Women are astonishing. 'That's a poor threat, though,' I remarked, 'seeing that you don't seem very anxious to speak to me again anyhow.'

'Oh, no, Robert.' She smiled at me. 'I have always intended to be a friend of yours.'

'That's kind of you. I didn't know that.'

'Perhaps you wouldn't have come here if you had.'

'Perhaps not.' It was my turn now to put on that little mocking smile. I hope I did put it on, and not some awful sickly grin. I suppose only women and actors can be sure about what their faces do for them.

'I must go now.' And she actually made for the door. I followed after her, quite slowly, determined that I wouldn't be the one to suggest a meeting this time.

I was, though.

But I will tell you about that later. You will say that there is too much chatter about the Masham in this letter, but I'm not sure if it is mere chatter. The ghost of an idea begins to haunt me, an idea that would be of immense service to you, my moonstruck lad. But more of that later. Meanwhile, can't you clutch young Rossett by the hair, get to the bottom of his affairs, and then either return here or get Jean to join you in town? Tell me what you would like me to do.

Yours,
ROBERT.

THE BROWN BULL.

MY DEAR MARK,

No more news from you yet. No matter. I am writing this (it's early evening) to try and get rid of my bad temper. Yes, I'm in a thoroughly bad temper.

I told you in my last that I had arranged to meet Marjorie. We were to meet at the little bridge on the first fine day. To-day was beautiful – a morning full of crisp sunlight, a day like a nut – and off I went, in high spirits, to the little bridge, which is, as you probably know, a couple of hours' sharp walking from here. I enjoyed every minute of the walk, and enjoyed the pipe I had at the bridge at the end of it. I didn't know definitely that Marjorie would be there, but was fairly confident she would turn up.

I had another pipe, and when that was finished I began to scan the road rather anxiously. It was now lunch-time and she was nowhere in sight. I was hungry too. Finally, I gave her up, sat me down by the side of the bridge, and pulled out my sandwiches.

'How greedy of you, Robert!' It was Marjorie, springing from nowhere. She made me spill three sandwiches, which I promptly offered to her.

'I'm better off than you are,' she remarked, and produced a basket of food and a thermos flask. It was a regular lunch.

'I'll never believe you've carried all those things all the way down Lambdale,' I told her. 'I believe you've come in the car.' And so she had, or at least the lunch had.

But I must speed up the narrative. We began eating and swopped egg sandwiches for tomato in the friendliest fashion. We didn't say much at first. I at least felt we didn't need to. It was a glorious day, and the whole setting made a wonderful background for Marjorie, who looks at her best in such places and at such times as these. I have given up wanting things to go on for ever, but it was nearly as good as that.

'Do you remember,' I asked, when we had nearly finished, 'that lunch we had on Cader Idris?' That was just after we were married, and one of our great memories, part of a day that was all pure gold.

'I remember being there,' said Marjorie coolly, 'but I don't remember lunch. Was there something special about it? Was it very bad or very good? – you get both in Wales.' And she turned a too wide and too innocent look upon me.

'It was very good,' I said, nettled. 'But I wasn't thinking of the food.'

'Oh, what were you thinking of?'

'Oh, nothing, nothing!' I was annoyed now, especially as I had looked round and caught the ghost of a smile vanishing. She wasn't playing the game.

We finished our meal in silence. Then I lit a pipe, and Marjorie found a cigarette for herself. The sun seemed to grow stronger, and the whole lovely place was aglow. We sat there, lazily smoking, basking in the sunlight.

'Isn't it beautifully warm now?' she said at last.

I said it was.

We were silent again for a minute or two, then she said softly: 'Do you remember that long, long afternoon we spent on Dartmoor, just sitting like this?'

Of course I did, because that was another of our great days. But it was my turn now, and for the life of me I couldn't resist it. 'No, I can't say I do,' I remarked easily. 'I seem to have had so many long afternoons.'

'What an insufferable remark, Robert!'

'Well, Marjorie, I——'

But then we both looked at one another and laughed. Now we were friends. We moved rather cautiously into serious talk. I won't repeat what we said. It is sufficient that we both owned we had been in the wrong. We were cool, you know, but friendly, distinctly friendly. There was, of course, still some distance for us both to go, much ground to recover. But we both made tremendous admissions.

'I can, I know,' said Marjorie, 'carry the spirit of independence to a length that becomes morbid. That sounds silly, but you know what I mean.' And I did.

'And I for my part,' I put in, 'can be quite insufferably intolerant, priggish, snobbish.'

'You can,' she replied, with alarming readiness.

'I'm willing to admit,' I went on, 'that I was wrong in the affair of Mrs Masham. I didn't treat her properly.'

'You mean,' she said, with emphasis, 'you didn't treat me properly.'

'Certainly, if you like. I didn't treat you properly. But I was thinking at the moment of my attitude towards Mrs Masham, which began all the trouble.'

'Oh, no, it didn't,' she put in. 'The trouble really began long before that.'

'Perhaps it did, but that affair brought it to a head. And I realise now,' I continued, warming to the work, 'that my attitude towards Mrs Masham was altogether too intolerant. You were right and I was wrong.'

'Splendid, Robert!' she murmured.

'Yes,' I said, 'you were right. I was too hasty, and I misjudged the woman. What right had I, who didn't know her, to sit in judgment upon her like that! I know her better now, and, although I can't pretend that she's one of the Heaven-born few, either very wise or very witty, I do see that she's a harmless, amiable creature, good at heart and rather pathetic, and certainly not to be despised by so frail a fellow-creature as myself.'

She looked at me, with raised eyebrows. 'My dear, there's no need to be abject. I don't want you to begin perjuring yourself. You know very well that she's a very silly, selfish, greedy old woman.'

I saw a trap here. I was not going to walk into it. 'No, no. Don't be sarcastic, Marjorie. I'm admitting that I was wrong. I don't know that she's any of those things, and now I freely admit I don't. You were right.'

'Oh, don't keep telling me I was right!' she cried. 'It's maddening. I'm not trying to be sarcastic; I leave that to you. I tell you she *is* a silly, selfish, greedy old woman; she's absolutely insufferable. If you knew what I've had to put up with——!'

'You're being grossly unfair now, Marjorie,' I told her.

'Of course! I'm being unfair! I'm wrong! As soon as I make a remark I'm still wrong, though you've been telling me how right I always am.' She was rapidly losing her temper now.

'But don't you see,' I began, reasonably enough, 'that if you are right now, then you were wrong then, and if you were right then, then you are wrong now——'

She put her hands to her ears and fairly shrieked. 'Oh, stop, stop! You're worse than ever, Robert. You've not learned anything.'

'I am being perfectly reasonable,' I said. I was annoyed myself now.

She jumped to her feet. 'You are being ridiculous,' she remarked icily.

'But you must see——' I began, but she cut me short.

'It's going to rain,' she said. And sure enough, great clouds were gathering, just as if our idiocies had suddenly reached up to the very skies. 'Would you mind helping me to put these things together?'

I did, and in complete silence. In the face of that gigantic unreason, there was nothing for me to say. A few drops fell on us. The thought that we were both about to be drenched gave me a certain pleasure. But then I heard the sound of a car coming up from Garrowdale.

'Hello, what's this?' I cried.

Marjorie looked down the road. 'Oh, that's Mrs Masham's car returning. I shall go back with it, as it's so threatening. Perhaps you had better come too. I'm sure your friend Mrs Masham will only be too delighted to see you.'

'I'll be hanged if I will!' I said, watching the car draw up to us.

Marjorie gave the flask and the basket to the chauffeur. 'I hope you don't get *too* wet, Robert,' she said, and then climbed in, leaving me staring.

And that was that. And I did get very wet indeed, absolutely soaked to the skin. And though I am now warm and dry and it is nearly dinnertime, I am still in a bad temper. Yes, of course, it's all very funny, and by the time I see you again I may be ready to exchange grins with you over it. But for the moment – No.

I have no other news and am waiting for yours.

ROBERT.

20 JERMYN STREET.
MY DEAR BOB,
   A very brief note just to tell you that Jean has arrived. She is in
London. Not only that, but at once she wrote to me saying that she was
staying with some cousin or other – a Miss Carey, 31 Muffet Street,
Bloomsbury, is the address – and that she would like to see me as soon as
it was convenient to me. 'As soon as it was convenient to me!' It was all I
could do not to rush off that very second to Bloomsbury, but I held
myself in – partly because now that she has taken this step I don't want to
frighten her by any impetuosity, and partly because young Rossett is
coming to see me this afternoon, and I want to get the naked truth out
of him (not that I shall, of course) before I see her. She could persuade
me to anything, even possibly to regarding her young brother with
charity, and I don't want to see him with any charity at all this afternoon.
   So I have sent a note by messenger to Bloomsbury telling her that I am
at her service (written quite coldly, I assure you, and as though I were her
solicitor or something) and asking her to lunch with me to-morrow here.
That she should actually eat and drink in this room, alone with me, isn't
it incredible? Aren't all my dreams coming true? Am I wrong to persuade
myself that she would never have come to London *only* because she
wanted to help her brother? She *must* be thinking of me a little or she
would never have written to me so soon after arriving. This Miss Carey.
Is she good to her, careful of her, thoughtful of her, or is she one of those
spidery, bony, chilly virgin relations who grudge every bite that you eat
and put only one blanket on your bed?
   I'm writing to you, Bob, wildly, any sort of fashion. The relief it is to
me to have someone to talk to, someone I care for and can trust! Do you
know what a lonely devil I have always been? I've only realised it during
these last months since I've written these letters to you. I've never written
intimately to anyone before: it was my need to talk about Jean that first
made me break out, but through the doing of it something quite new for
me has come out of it. Something not to do with Jean at all. I've grown
closer to you in my absence from you than I ever did when I was with
you. I suspect that there are millions of people who could make a
friendship through writing that they never could in actual speech. Let
them try it and see! Maybe it's brought something fearful on to your
head. I shall never get free of the habit of writing to you now – but you

can always burn them unread. That's the best of letters. There's never any compulsion on one to answer.

It's one of London's smoky mornings to-day. It's as though in another minute everything will break into flame. And through the smoke there's a rattle-rattle as though everyone knew the fire was coming and were packing up as fast as they could. The man's come to clear the breakfast things. He's just like Horatio Bottomley with a lisp and a high voice. He speaks like a chorus-lady being very genteel at a party. If he talks to me again about the gentlemen he's known I shall throw the inkpot at him.

Yours,
MARK.

20 JERMYN STREET

DEAR BOB,

Young Rossett has been and has gone, and the odd thing is that I don't
want to fumigate the room or even open the windows. I'm more on his
side than ever I could have supposed possible. No, not on his side. That –
with his attitude to Jean and life in general – I could never be! But he's
put his case without in the least being aware of it. He's been honest for
once, and it's all the same to him as his dishonesty. He doesn't positively
know which is which.

He came in like a hunted rat. He begged me to give him a whisky,
which I did. He was past all consciousness of dislike of myself; he didn't
think of me at all except as a possible means of escape. He's reached, after
every sort of conceivable twisting and turning, an absolute blank wall.
He's run to earth. The chase is over.

I told him at once that the only hope of getting my aid was to be
ruthlessly honest. I said that nothing that he could tell me would shock
me, so he'd better come out with all of it. So he did. Or at any rate with
most of it. I suppose that fellows like this never come out with *all* of it,
it's so ingrained in them to keep something back. There's always at the
end of their mind that it's cleverer to tell lies than the truth – this desire
to 'put it over' someone will never leave them until the breath's out of
their body – but so far as he could he told me everything.

It didn't, after all, amount to an awful lot. It began, I suppose, years
and years ago up at Farthing Hall (how that odd house seems to be at the
back of every side of this little story!), when he, a miserable peaky little
boy with no stamina, a natural tendency to lie and steal, trembled before
his father's tempers and drank with the stable boy and flirted with the
kitchenmaid. He had desires and never any money to satisfy them with.
He hated the country. *That*, I imagine, is the real key to the whole
situation. Everything that was religion to his father – the house, the
valley, the hills, the old stories and legends, all the pride of place and
family, was nauseating to him. He hated the damp and dullness and
country sights and sounds. He liked to bet on a horse, but was terrified of
riding one. Keswick was the nearest he could get to gaiety, and he
stepped over there whenever he could, but that wasn't so easy, and meant
beatings when he returned. I have a fancy that if he'd been another type
of boy – sporting, honest and friendly, with an affection for his land – the

history both of himself and his father would have been quite different. That old Rossett that you've seen – a rather genial, kindly, warmhearted old boy – would, through pride and love of his son, have developed and grown. But how could any father take pride in this miserable little pipsqueak? Well, he got into every kind of mess and trouble at home, was never sent to school as he should have been, and then at eighteen or so, because he was such a nuisance at home, won his desire and was sent on some job to London.

The sequence is, of course, clear enough. Drink, women, debt, money-lenders, lies, ill-health, and then I daresay (although he wouldn't own to it), worse things, nearly landing him, if all were known, in the tender clutches of the law. In any case that's what he's terrified of now. He sees jail staring at him. Some years back he met Mulligan, the fat, white-faced, lady-pursuing gentleman of whom I've written already. Mulligan lives, it appears, on poor creatures like Rossett, and makes, I should think, quite a fair thing out of it. What hold exactly Mulligan has over the boy I don't know – forgery is part of it, I imagine. In any case Mulligan is Rossett's hell on earth. He haunts him morning and night. He can't escape him wherever he goes. The very mention of Mulligan sends him into a blue fit. He sweats Mulligan at every pore.

And so – you'll wonder, Bob, that at this point I didn't tear the dear boy into little pieces and throw him out of the window – he has been approaching ever more nearly the dirtiest and beastliest moment of his history, namely, that he should assist Mulligan to be friendly with Jean. That is the way he put it. Even he didn't quite dare to put all the consequences into words. Mulligan has met Jean several times, and given young Rossett to understand that 'if he can make it all right with his sister,' he, Mulligan, will 'make it all right' with young Rossett.

At this point I didn't waste words by explaining to friend Rossett exactly what he was. No words, or even blows of mine, would have affected him in the least. He had gone far beyond me into regions of darkness and terror where I could never follow him. Nor did I have much opportunity. He broke suddenly (and without in the least knowing that he was doing it) into a kind of *Apologia pro vita sua*.

His notion was that he'd never for a moment been given a square deal. He'd been surrounded from the first by people who didn't understand him. He'd been forced from the beginning to regard himself as a fool and a weakling. Because he wasn't like his father, because he hated sport and the open air and the country (that hatred being born in him and not his fault at all), he'd been bullied and kicked and despised. Well, I asked him, what *had* he cared for? What would he have done if he'd been given a chance?

Oh, mechanics – anything to do with machinery. He'd have been a nailer at that if he'd been given half an opportunity. No one understood a motor car better than he did, and years ago, before motor cars were the thing, it had been the same. Anything to do with machinery. But everybody and everything had been against him. Jean came into this too. She had ruined him by her fine silly ideas about him, thinking him noble and high-minded and all the rest of it. Of course he wasn't noble. He was just like any other chap. Who ever heard of anyone being noble with the sort of father he had? If only they'd let him alone! If ten years ago he'd been given a pound or two and shoved into some sort of contact with machinery, he'd be as good as any of them. But he'd never had any luck, not a shadow of any.

And so, perhaps, he hasn't. Who's to say? Not myself anyway. 'There but for the Grace of God——' However, he hadn't much time to consider his case, and I hadn't either. I didn't tell him that Jean was here. He thinks she's still in Cumberland. The shadow of Mulligan is upon him. You can see that great greasy swine moving as he moves. Something has got to be done and that quickly.

The boy cried at the last, hateful, terrified, broken-down sobbing. I couldn't stand that, and got rid of him, promising that something should be done. But what? There's a world here, Bob, that's outside my knowledge. I may easily blunder now in the steps I take. I'm moving in the dark. But – Jean comes to-morrow – and with her beside me I'm ready for anything!

Affectionately,

MARK.

THE BROWN BULL.

MY DEAR MARK,

Many thanks for your two letters. I heard that Jean had gone, but didn't see her myself again before she left. The man Mulligan, considered soberly in the light of Garrowdale, seems as remote as a pterodactyl. Things at your end appear to be in a pretty mess, and though I don't frankly consider myself much use in dealing with such messes, I am, of course, at your service. Say the word and I will be with you within twenty-four hours or less.

The only thing I can do for you, I am doing. I am keeping old Rossett amused. I believe if I were not here, he would at once pack an antique Gladstone and descend upon you all in London, and what would happen then I leave you to imagine. (Though I should like to see him knock Mulligan down, which he certainly would do as soon as he set eyes on the creature.) He is the only thing that has been happening here. Marjorie I haven't seen since our last absurd dispute at the bridge. I know she is still in Lambdale, though, a fact that gives me comfort. Mrs Masham I have seen once, and talked to her again about Rossett. Indeed, she came round to the subject quite briskly. She wants to buy some land about here.

Which brings me again to Rossett, who has been in and out a good deal these last two or three days. The first time he came, he was furiously angry, an ancestral voice prophesying woe. His son was a groggy-kneed pimp, his daughter a half-witted little madam, who wanted to go trapesing after him, and so on and so forth. He began to abuse you, until I lost patience, told him that you were a friend of mine, and that he was talking nonsense. Then the storm fell upon me. He stood there, towering over me and glaring down, the veins standing out on his forehead. He called me a damned fool.

'Good-morning,' I said, as coolly as I could, and turned away. I must say I expected that great fist of his to land on the back of my neck as I walked to the door. When I got to the door, I looked back at him. He was still standing there, glaring. Confound him, I thought, I must have a parting shot. 'We haven't a telephone here,' I said.

'I don't want a telephone,' he bellowed. 'D'you think I want to call the police?'

'No,' I remarked. 'A chemist's.' And left him staring.

But in the evening he came over and, now quite subdued and rather apologetic, begged me to dine with him. Jean must have gone then, and the elderly female must have retired to her bed for several days, for we were alone. As he filled himself with liquor, self-pity oozed out of him. He'd begun life with everything in his favour, but things had gone wrong. His wives had died. His two children had disappointed him. (Even Jean had no real spirit, he complained, completely overlooking the fact that every time she had given the slightest sign of having a mind and will of her own, he had raged and stormed at her.) His grand old estate was rapidly going to pieces; he was up to his neck in mortgages and debts. The world of to-day was no place for a gentleman. The times were out of joint.

With the brandy − that drink of heroes − he suddenly cheered up, turned to the good old times, and reeled off a kind of epic of rural amours, vast potations, and feuds. He told me a thing or two about his illegitimate offspring, one of whom − once a wild lad and a great favourite − is now the mate of a tramp steamer. And he ended by giving me a long and detailed account of an affair he had had with a certain pretty widow of Penrith, quite an admirable *conte drolatique*, I assure you. When I found myself at my own door, and turned back for a moment to look at Farthing Hall, a squat shape, but only faint in the thin moonlight, it seemed to be a ghost from a past century, a house sinking back, huddling down, into long-lost years. A queer evening.

Yesterday he came across just after Mrs Masham had departed in her car. 'Was that the woman from Lambdale?' he asked.

I told him it was and that she had told me she was thinking of buying some land hereabouts.

He whistled at this. 'What's she want to buy land here for?' he growled. 'No good to her. Rich, isn't she?'

'Very,' I said. 'Rich enough to buy us all out.'

'What does she want here?'

'Wants to settle here, at least for part of every year. Has fallen in love with the country. She's a lonely woman and can afford to gratify all her whims.'

He whistled again. 'Damned shame that a woman like that should have all that money! No real use for it! Good old families all over the place having to sell out, and women like that——' He blew out his breath and snapped his fingers. 'Why doesn't she come and ask *my* advice if she wants to know something about the land here? If there's any man knows more than I do, I'd like to meet him.'

'She wants to,' I said, with the quiet earnest manner of the accomplished liar, 'but she's afraid of you. She knows that you can tell her more than anybody else, but she's afraid you might resent it − for she was telling me how much she sympathises with the few remaining members of the old families, the really old families – and also because she seems to be afraid of you personally.'

'Why, what have I done?' roared the old ruffian indignantly. 'I'm a gentleman, aren't I! No lady need be afraid of meeting me.'

'Of course not. But when I asked her why she was afraid of meeting you, she seemed embarrassed, and so I changed the subject. You know' – I added, very fatuously – 'what women are.'

You should have seen him standing there, turning this over in his mind, an idiotic conceited dawn breaking on his face. Finally he said: 'Well, well, well! But this Mrs Masham knows nothing about me; she's only seen me twice.'

'As I think I mentioned before,' I told him, 'she has heard a great deal. She is probably studying the history of the neighbourhood——'

'Not all its history, I hope. Haw-haw!' And he poked me in the ribs. He must have been thinking of the widow of Penrith – and others.

'No, not all. Ha-ha!' I returned, a companion ass. Then I looked grave (and probably even more asinine) and said: 'Also, as I mentioned before, I think she has a tremendous opinion of you. But let's change the subject.'

The ancient wheeze, redolent of the gas and oranges of a hundred old theatres, quite succeeded. Hastily he waved away any possible change of subject, held up his hand, opened his mouth to speak, thought better of it, was silent a few moments, suddenly looked anxious, and asked: 'Anybody acting for her in all this land-buying business?'

I hadn't the least idea, but by this time I was clean out of earshot of all conscience. I racked my brains to find the name of those local lawyers and estate people who figured in so many of his tales as the villains of the piece. 'I think it's – wait a minute – yes, it is – you know the people – Frog – something——'

'Not those scoundrels, Frodsham and Frent,' he shouted. 'They're the biggest rogues between Carlisle and Preston, and that little swine Frent hates me like the devil. I believe they've got paper of mine too. Why, they'll persuade her to buy this very dale if she'll listen to them, half the old Farthing Hall estate at least. And it could be done too, damn it. They could buy the mortgages as cheap as rotten apples. I can see 'em foreclosing. They'd like nothing better. Why, Frent's the fellow I knocked down in his own office.' He went striding up and down the room. 'This is a devil of a mess, Newlands, a devil of a mess.'

'I'm sure Mrs Masham would do nothing,' I began mumbling, to give him his cue.

'I must see her,' he announced. 'I must put a stop to this, one way or another. She seems to be a decent sort of woman, though silly in her ideas——'

'A widow, you know,' I put in. 'Nothing to do and too much money to spend.'

'I know, I know. And she's obviously got some sense, from what you tell me. I must say I didn't dislike the look of her at all. I like a fine figure of a woman, none of your weedy sexless hags. It 'ud be a sin to let a woman like that get into the hands of such sharks as Frodsham and Frent. Newlands,' – and here he clapped me on the back – 'we must go over there together, soon as possible. To-morrow. Don't want to walk, though. Perhaps that car of hers would take us again. What about getting a message through?'

So we arranged to go. That was yesterday, but it was too late to get a message through for to-day. Early to-morrow morning, however, the car comes for us, and I shall see Marjorie and Rossett will see his Mrs Masham. And if something wonderful doesn't happen, then I am no prophet.

If you are saying to yourself (between bouts with Mulligan): 'What is he telling me all this stuff for?' – then you are both an ungrateful and a dense young man. I tell you the whole plot is thickening, and in the very thickest little bit you will find – of all people——

Yours *ex machina*,
ROBERT.

20 JERMYN STREET.

MY DEAR BOB,

Your letter has come with your news about old Rossett. I can't help it; your squabbles and Farthing Hall and the crinkly hills and the running stream are all as unreal to me as everything else is to-night. My very room is unreal; these shabby cushions shine with burning gold, and the fireplace encloses a huddle of magic fire, and the curtains blowing faintly in the wind are secret messages from the moon. I can't help it. I wouldn't if I could. The desire of my life is come, the greatest happiness possible to man is upon me and is grasped by me and realised. Jean loves me and I love Jean, and nothing else in this strange place is true.

She loves me and she won't marry me – not until her father and brother are out of her responsibility. She says that she is a fool, that she has always been a fool, that she knows that they don't want her, that they are both sick to death of her, that they can get on quite well without her – nevertheless she can't leave them, and until something satisfactory comes of them she won't marry me.

She is so absolutely old-fashioned, in look, in voice, in simple directness of mind and heart and soul, that any sensible modern person would be out of patience with her completely. I have discovered that I am not modern myself in any way. My passion for Manet ought to have shown that long ago, but liking Dufresne and Gen Paul and Friez and one or two other French painters blinded me perhaps.

I know now that I died in 1870 and so did Jean. We are happy ghosts visiting a world of wireless and mechanical hares. I kissed her just after Horatio Bottomley had dropped upon the table two of the most loathsome congealing chops and, with a shrill feminine sigh, departed. I, happy ghost, kissed her ghostly eyes and her ghostly hair and so we stayed, letting the chops congeal still further. And she? She is a friend of Lily Dale and Mrs Gaskell's Mollie, and has been bored by Jane Eyre.

Taking me by the hand she showed me, out of the window, Dizzy moving down St James's and the Prince Consort brushing his hair, and an elderly gentleman with side-whiskers stopping under a lamp-post to study the new number of *Bleak House*. Then, with a sigh, she leapt into my heart and stayed there comfortably resting.

But ghosts can be in two places at once, so, the chops neglected, we walked out, unperceived by man, flew through the golden air and alighted in Oxford Street. How often has that other Me (now so happily deceased) loathed Oxford Street! How has he detested those grimy shop windows filled with incredible gloves, unsanctified corsets, unbelievable boots and shoes (although in the midst of these he was forced, that dim, almost vanished reality, to confess that here, too, was the best book-shop in London). And those crowds, so restlessly searching for something that will be cheaper than anything ever was before and not minding its nastiness! And the weather, always mud and rain in Oxford Street and cross umbrellas poking one another in the eye, and the Salvation Army for ever beating its drum round the corner! That's how it was to vanished reality — but now (for happy ghosts have ever a transmuting eye) everything swims in gold, the gutters run red wine, and crimson flamingos are perched on the chimney-tops. And as we walked we talked as only ghosts can talk. When had she loved me first? That time in the lane, when I had stood before her and threatened her very life. Oh yes, she had known it then, although she had not admitted it. How could she admit it with all the difficulties that there were, and she had been alone so long, how could she suppose that anyone would ever want her? And this other ghost, when had he . . .? What! That first moment at the theatre? Ah, impossible! That was madness, after so short a glimpse. And then one ghostly hand touched another, and all the crimson flamingos came sweeping down upon Oxford Street and perched on the hats of the pushing, perspiring shoppers, and the shoppers were suddenly aware of a new light in the air and an ease and spaciousness, and an old lady who had been hesitating about buying a shawl for her old sister went in at once and bought one that cost twice as much as she had thought to pay for it. And the taxi-men offered to take customers for nothing, and all the policemen grew wings and flew in a cloud to Selfridge's.

Did we talk of the ghost's young brother or tiresome, obstreperous old father? Only this word about the old 'un, that — seen with ghostly eyes of tenderness, pity and love — he was a dear, and, if only left with one foot on his native heath and the other in the cradle of his ancestors, nobody could be nicer. Seen with ghostly eyes he was a heroic figure, the last of a noble race, longing to be loved, loyal to his blood — and so, dear, unghostly friend, I pray you to see him. Nor, at present, let him know that his daughter loves the loathsome young painter whom he hurled from his windows. But never mind. A fig for parents, a grape-fruit for ancestors! I sit here writing to you, and my heart pounds through my thumbs; I see angels in the ceiling, and all Donatello's choir-boys singing up the chimney.

She loves me, and when I've thrown father into the moon (which is streaming through the windows like a tipsy new penny) and tumbled brother into the basement of the London Museum, we are going to take a barouche into Cumberland, ask all the tenants to a dinner and dance Sir Roger down the lane.

If we have dived into 1840 don't fish us up again. Let us lie among the wax fruit under the gleaming candelabra and so pass into eternity.

Yours, in love with all the world,

MARK.

20 JERMYN STREET.

DEAR BOB,

Things are moving swiftly — so fast indeed that I am unable to believe that this is *my* life or *my* personality or *my* anything — except Jean, who is mine, mine for ever, let the low gin-and-bitter world that I'm in now move as it may.

My world moves round Mulligan, and Mulligan is the god of it. I had a talk with him last night which intrigued me so vastly that I'm sorry I can only give you the fringe of it. I wish that one of those fellows who write real honest-to-God novels would let me introduce him to Mulligan and then, being introduced, live with him, eat with him, sleep under the same roof with him for a year of Sundays. You remember Verloc in *The Secret Agent*, how he looked as though he'd wallowed, all day, on an unmade bed? Well, that's Mulligan's world. You know how sometimes one reads in our splendid daily press about some fellow who's been a spy for the Soviet or a blackmailer or a pimp, and suddenly all the melodramas of Oppenheim and Wallace are as realistic as gas-light. 'Why,' we say, 'I've been thinking that that world was Martian, and here it is right at my elbow.' That's how I feel about Mulligan.

Not that our talk last night was a very long one. I went to young Rossett's night club again and sat once more at the dreary little table and listened to the black-faced dreary little band. But this time the room was crowded and with *what* figures — figures all in two dimensions cut out of tissue paper, moving like somnambulists to the tune of 'I'm going to die to-morrow, I am.' The girl who asked me to marry her was there again and at once made for me. She finds me fascinating. In her half-dead mourning way she told me so, explaining once more that if I would only see her now and then she would be very grateful and would repay me in kind. When I asked her in what kind, she replied that she could tell me a thing or two that would make me want to water my eyebrows. About Mulligan, I asked her? Could she tell me anything about Mulligan? Could she not? With no excitement nor indeed emotion of any kind she told me that she could make me sick with Mulligan, and that if I wanted to have details about the *vie intime* of the devil her little facts about Mulligan would give me all I needed.

Then Mulligan himself appeared, rather neatly dressed in dinner jacket, white waistcoat, and glassy gardenia. I went right up to him and said that

I would like a word with him. For a moment I am happy to say I frightened him. He couldn't at the first instant place me, and he lives, I suppose, in a perpetual apprehension of any complete stranger, never knowing when the blow will fall. In an instant, however, after a glance at me, he recovered; he could see I wasn't the type to have any inside knowledge of him.

He thought, I fancy, that I was some young ass in trouble, who had heard that he had money to lend (at a very pretty interest), or trusted to his inside acquaintance with every sort of roguery. He was quite courteous, and came to my table, ordered a drink, and then regarded me with the kindly, benevolent air of a bishop at a garden-party. What could he do for me? What he could do for me, I explained immediately, was to let my young friend Rossett go. Whatever hold he had over the boy he was to loosen and that speedily. I wore quite a brave, determined air over this. Carrying Jean with me wherever I go has made me brave.

His manner altered at once. I could see that he was asking himself at once how much did I know, what was behind my confidence. I'm glad at least that he never realised how little I *did* know. He became grand, dominating. He visibly swelled before my eyes. I saw that he had a vast pride in his power, that it was the one god that he worshipped – outside women, of course – and that all the little, mean, dirty, vile, cruel tricks with which his life was filled were, in the light of his consciousness of his power, grand, magnificent acts like Bismarck plunging France and Germany into war or Napoleon and his whiff of grape-shot.

I tried to take as determined a stand as I could, but I wasn't very successful. In the first place, I knew too little of what Rossett had really done and was afraid of showing it, and, in the second place, the room bewildered me with its smell of drains and face-powder, its dim lights and shadowy, ghostly, meandering bodies. Then the man himself dominated me. I realised suddenly that, in his conceit of himself, no villainy was impossible for him, that he felt no one's misery, cared for no one's tears, had as little remorse as a boa-constrictor. To take me up and break me across his knee was no more for him than to drink a Vermouth, and I could imagine how quickly after doing it he would have me shovelled away into a corner and that the band would only play the louder.

He asked me quietly what I wanted him to do about Rossett, and why was I interested. I said that I knew the boy and was a friend of the family. A friend of the family? His interest livened. He was thinking, I suppose, of Jean. Oh, well, in that case if I was a friend of the family I must realise how good he had been to the boy, how much the boy owed to him. He swelled with virtue. If it hadn't been for him. . . . Had he not done this or that . . . where would the boy be now? In jail, of course, and plenty of it at that.

He talked to me like a father, wondered how anyone who was a real friend of the family could have allowed the boy to go the way he was going. Why had I not tried to save the boy from evil companions, loose women and so on? Did I not see . . . ? But I broke in upon this humbug, asked him if anything was to be gained by such nonsense, asked him at last if it was money that he wanted. He smiled, a confidential, friendly smile. No, it was not money. He didn't want to lose the boy. He told me frankly that he liked to have the boy ready at his side, and I saw his big white fingers close and unclose and his mouth opened ever so slightly and his red tongue touched the lips as though he were tasting something pleasant.

What he wanted – he suddenly got up, stood over me, swelling with fat under his clothes, his cheeks puffing, his eyes slipping into his head. What he wanted – well, if I were a friend of the family perhaps I would help him to know the family too. The boy had a sister, a nice girl. Now, why shouldn't I be friendly and amiable? Why shouldn't we all be friends together? Why not? He looked at me, smiling.

'You can find me here most evenings,' he said. 'If you want to help the boy, bring the girl,' then strutted, his head up, into the room, picked up some attendant damsel and vanished, dancing like a walloping elephant.

So, Bob, it goes. Or rather doesn't go. But I'm in the thick of it. I won't stop or stay until I have my hand at Mulligan's heart and can feel it stop its beating from fear. Sheer Oppenheim or that Clubfoot gentleman. Never mind. Jean's at the end of it.

Affectionately,
MARK.

PINE HOUSE,
LAMBDALE.

MY DEAR MARK,

This is going to be a dreadful scrawl, and I'm afraid there may be a lot of it. You must do your best with it. You see, such a lot has happened. I'm at Mrs Masham's – you came here once yourself, didn't you? – and am horizontal almost. I'm nursing a ferocious ankle, and am still fagged out, though garrulous, after an adventure up in the mountains. It's been a crazy business.

Rossett and I came here quite early the morning of the day before yesterday. The car brought us. As soon as I saw Mrs Masham, she told me that Marjorie had set out to climb Wetherfell, which she and I had once climbed together. I didn't know if Marjorie had gone to escape meeting me or to make a fantastic rendezvous with me in the clouds (and she didn't know either, she has since told me), but I set out after her, at least as soon as Mrs Masham had given me a few sandwiches. It wasn't a bad morning, a fair mixture of sun and cloud, and about three hours' hard walking and scrambling, over Long Mell and then Green End, I knew would bring me to the very top of Wetherfell. She had been gone about an hour and a half before, and I thought I might catch her at the summit or on the way back, perhaps at Mell Hause, where so many tracks meet and there is a shelter and where you always come across somebody you know. It's 2,500 feet up, good old Mell Hause, and one of the most God-forsaken spots in this island, yet I know no place except the club and the Queen's Hall where I am likely to meet more people I know. (But not at this time of the year, though: I was forgetting that.)

Off I went, then. There's only one way from Lambdale to the top of Wetherfell, and I knew I couldn't miss her. I pushed on over Long Mell, dipped into the valley, then up to Green End. From there the track goes down again, then climbs up to Mell Hause (which you mustn't miss or you get tied up among some very nasty crags, deep gullies, and steep slopes rotten with scree). From Mell Hause the way up to Wetherfell is marked with cairns, and in places there's a pretty drop at each side. Forgive this guidebook stuff, but I want you to understand what happened, at least to understand as much as I do.

From the top of Green End I could see far ahead, but couldn't spot Marjorie. I hurried down into the valley and promised myself that I would lunch at Mell Hause. By the time I had reached the bottom of the valley, I noticed that the sun was going and the sky flopping down, but it didn't look too bad. I kept my nose down more or less on the long drag up towards Mell Hause. The first half is far steeper than the second, which is almost like a plateau. At 2,000 feet quite suddenly I walked into a thick mist. It dropped like a blanket on the whole mountain-side. You know what it's like – at one minute you're in a definite place and are going to another definite place, are comfortably on a map; and the very next minute you're nowhere, lost in a spectral world, clean off the map. If I had been going on an ordinary little climb, I should have turned back then and there. But Marjorie was somewhere ahead and much worse off than I was, so of course I went on. And equally of course I hadn't a compass, and I knew that Marjorie would not have one.

It was very slow going now, with only about a couple of yards of track visible, not an inch more. Still I made some sort of progress. 'Mell Hause for lunch,' I told myself, and even said it aloud just to break the mournful silence. I came to the conclusion I must be about a mile away. But then there came a rocky bit, no path, with the way marked with tiny cairns – you know the kind of thing. When you came to one of these little pyramids, it was just possible to see the next one ahead – and that was all. Well, I had done about a hundred yards or so in this fashion when suddenly I discovered that there weren't any more cairns. Nor was I off the rocks and back again on a path. I moved very cautiously a few yards in what seemed to me the right direction, and found myself looking into nothing, with mist almost beneath my very feet. Here was some sort of precipice: it might be fifty feet deep or five hundred, I couldn't tell. Obviously I had got off the track, having mistaken a triangular-shaped rock for a cairn. (I've done it before.) I turned my back on the chasm and spent several minutes scrambling over the slippery rocks. No cairns to be seen at all. Finally I saw a dark mass in front, and found myself facing a great wall of rock, disappearing into the mist. I was now absolutely lost. It may sound silly, but if you have been in one of these mists you will know how difficult it is. I was as helpless as if I had just been dropped upon a strange planet.

I followed this wall of rock round to the left, which I knew was away from the chasm, and finally came to the end of it or what I thought was the end of it. Like a fool, I plunged forward and upward, over loose scree at first and then more steeply up steps of wet rock. The place darkened, and then I saw that I had got into a kind of crack in the wall, a chimney. The last dozen yards were very nasty indeed, but at last I pulled myself up to the top, where the mist was thicker than ever, and I seemed to be on a ledge. There were a few square yards of rock under my feet and that was all; I could see nothing in any direction but swirling mist. I sat down and tried to think it out.

Then the mist began to swirl more violently until at last a great wind came and blew a hole in it. I caught glimpses of sunlit grass, at the end of a white tunnel, a thousand feet below. There came another tremendous gust that thinned the mist into faint smoke. Shapes came rushing through, and then for one half-minute the whole mountain-side was clear. I saw then that I was tangled up on the steep face of rock well to the right of Mell Hause. I ought to have remembered that the track, which I missed, swept round to the left to avoid this face. I was actually standing on a gleaming little ledge that ran upwards on the steep side. I had just time to see this before the mist settled again and blotted out everything. Very shakily I moved up to the left until the ledge narrowed to nothing. Here the rock was broken and not too steep, so I climbed very slowly. The top was a pretty sharp edge, part of a long narrow elbow. I worked away to the left, began to descend on the far side, sometimes slipping and sliding in a blue funk, until at last I realised I must be on the Mell Hause plateau. The little stone shelter couldn't be more than half a mile away, to the left.

I was more confident now, increased the pace, and of course rushed on to disaster. I had scrambled to the top of a big heap of boulders, when suddenly my legs went from under me and I shot forward. I only fell about ten feet, but I came down heavily, with one foot doubled under me and one side of my head and my right hand badly cut. When I tried to get up I shouted with pain. My right ankle seemed so much screaming pulp. It was agony to move it. I managed to loosen my boot-laces and then lay there, feeling dizzy and sick.

You can imagine what I felt. Many a better man than I has slid out of this life because he broke an ankle in such a place. Fortunately, I wasn't at the bottom of a chimney, but on reasonably level ground. My only chance was to move on somehow, to get nearer to the shelter, where Marjorie was probably waiting for the mist to clear. So I did move on – at the rate of a yard a minute on hands and knees. It was horrible, I can tell you. Sometimes I gave a shout, but it seemed futile to try and make any sound penetrate that damned white blanket of mist. After about an hour of this, I curled up and rested, eating a sandwich or two. Then I started again, a miserable thing of mud and blood and aching bones, crawling over wet rock. Once I thought I heard a vague shout, and stopped to listen for it again, stopped at least five minutes. A few more yards then brought me off the rocks, on to grass. I stood up and hopped a few paces, then fell down, exhausted by the effort. My ear, close to the ground, heard something, sounds of somebody moving. I gave another shout or two. I moved on again, towards the sound. A vague shape came through the mist towards me. It was Marjorie.

We managed to get to the stone shelter together, for it was not very far away. There we ate what was left of our food and I lay with my leg outstretched and my boot off, Marjorie having bathed the ankle. What we said to one another then cannot be told, not even to you, my dear Mark. We sat there close in a world that was nothing but rock and white mist, but we saw one another clearly enough at last. Both of us had been wrong – I more than she, with all my silly little arrogance – but now, in this desolation, we became simple again and talked to one another easily and quietly. I think that in that hour or two we built up even more than we had formerly destroyed. And somewhere in that stone shelter at Mell Hause there ought to be an old skin, sloughed off by the real Robert Newlands. Not a little of the man who has written so many letters to you lately, Mark, will be found shrivelling in that old skin.

But I must push on. This looks like being the very longest letter I have ever written, and Marjorie, who has just come in, says it is time I stopped scribbling. I have been granted another ten minutes, though, so here goes.

We waited in the shelter for the mist to go, and at last it did begin to disappear, but so too did the daylight. In an hour or two it would be completely dark, and I couldn't walk properly. Very soon too it would be bitterly cold. To spend a whole night in late autumn up there! – we began to look at one another. After much talk we decided to return while there was still some daylight left. My ankle was very painful and an enormous size; impossible to put my boot on again. We set out, however, and moved very slowly, for I could only hop and hobble and had to lean on Marjorie, who was very tired herself. We made lamentable progress and saw the daylight go ebbing out. We were on the right track, but it seemed hopeless. Marjorie still smiled but was white and trembling, and I could have whimpered with pain and exhaustion. We rested, struggled on again, rested, struggled on, while the whole mountain-side slipped into darkness.

Then we heard a voice calling across the valley from Green End. We made some sort of noise in reply. I could go no farther, but Marjorie hurried down the slope. I think I must have fallen into a kind of stupor for some ten minutes or so, perhaps much longer; but the next thing I remember is Rossett standing in front of me, with two other great fellows by his side. And – by thunder! – old Rossett may be a bad father, a quarrelsome neighbour, a boastful old ruffian, anything you like, but, let me tell you, he's the man to meet when you're lying out on a darkening fell with a rotten ankle! He's as strong as a horse and knows every inch of the ground. It seems he had watched the mist settling on the tops, guessed that it would stay till late afternoon, so that when we failed to return he knew at once what we were in for and set out to find us, taking two or three other fellows from Lambdale with him. It's not the first time he's been with search parties, as you may imagine, and he's an old hand. And, of course, he enjoyed every minute of it. Marjorie can tell you more about the latter part of the adventure than I can. It was very late indeed when I was finally slung into this house, and I spent all yesterday in bed, with some attention from a doctor called out from Keswick.

Rossett is still here – Mrs Masham insisted upon his staying – and is still triumphant, emperor of the fells. Marjorie is at my elbow now, and sends her love. We're both looking forward to your letters, if any are waiting for me at the Brown Bull. I shall be here for some days yet, for Mrs Masham, who has enjoyed all this too, more especially as it fulfils some dark prophecy made by one of her late visitors, will not hear of any of us stirring. So here we are, and I think I shall be able to let you have some amusing news soon, amusing, I say, but also of the utmost importance. You wait.

                                                              Yours,
                                                              ROBERT.

20 JERMYN STREET.

MY DEAR BOB,

I have just had your long letter describing your accident. I cannot tell you how alarmed at first it made me, but then I reflected that you were now safely in bed with about five hundred people to guard you and, above all, Marjorie to hold you down.

The reality of your adventure flung into bright relief the unreality of mine. You have really tumbled down and broken your ankle; I have been chasing Radcliffian shadows under modern dress.

It amuses me a little to speculate how it would have been if it had been Mulligan who had fallen down the mountain side and I who had found him. He would have been quite a lovable human being, I've no doubt, at any rate until Mrs Masham's maid brought him his morning tea, when I wouldn't have trusted him. But our two so opposite worlds do join somewhere, and I fancy that old Rossett and his house are the common ground. Shall I soon return to my normal pre-Jean kind of vision and no longer see men as trees walking? I have a kind of idea that I shall. I love Jean more with every minute of the day, but now that she is my companion both in body and soul, the fantasy of an elusive pursuit is subsiding and all the other fantasies are subsiding with it. This morning Mulligan and his 'Hand me over the girl' are gathering the grey ordinariness of a common police-court case. I want to get out of it all as soon as I can, go into the country somewhere, and start painting Jean.

After a week in the country I shall doubt Mulligan's very existence.

To return for a moment to your letter; I can't tell you how delighted I am that you and Marjorie are close together again, closer than you have ever been before.

Of course I knew that it must be so, but all this time I have been longing for you to be happy, and reading through the lines of your letters your deep distress.

But selfishly I suppose I must be grateful, because had you been happy you would not have written to me. Now that you are with Marjorie again, your letter-writing is over. I shall miss them more than you know.

Well, the young night-club lady who finds me fascinating has been to tea with me. Unchaperoned moreover. Her name is Dora Mellin. She arrived quite unembarrassed, as impassive as ever, and very quietly dressed with a little string of false pearls and a black silk dress.

She said (after discovering that I had no cocktails) that she would prefer whisky to tea, so it was whisky that she had. Then there she sat, in perfect propriety, as though she belonged to one of the good old county families, and regarded me with unblinking solemnity.

I came to the point at once. 'If you're really a friend of mine,' I said, 'I want you to tell me all you know about young Rossett and Mulligan.' She was disappointed. She wanted to tell me about herself, her first husband and how he'd beaten her. 'The odd thing about him was,' she remarked, 'that he was only decent to me when he was drunk, and he was sober most of the time.'

He was a little man with side-whiskers. He was 'something in the City'. When he was very sober indeed he stripped the clothes off her back, tied her to a bed-post, and beat her. He was a religious man apparently.

'Do you believe there's a God like he did?' she asked me. I answered that the word God could mean so many different things. 'It only meant one thing to him,' she answered. 'When he'd been extra mean, he saw God as clear as anything. God encouraged him in all the meanest things he did.'

Then happily the little side-whiskered man in the City faded out of sight and she jumped straight on to Mulligan. She didn't know exactly what the relations between him and Rossett were, but she did know that the silly young fool had forged a signature or two – something to do with motor cars, she fancied.

'What do you want to save the boy for?' she asked me. 'He was born a rotter, he'll always be a rotter. He's better in jail.'

I came out with it at once. I loved his sister. It was for her that I was doing this.

She sighed, flicked her cigarette ash into the fire, got up and stood looking out of the window at the chimney-pots. Then she turned round, her hand on her hip, and, looking at me, said: 'You're a good sort. Of course I never had a dog's chance with a fellow like you. But I don't care now. I haven't cared about anything for years. I'd marry young Rossett as soon as not. He makes me feel motherly, and he wouldn't beat me. I'd put him over my knee and smack his behind if he tried to.'

She looked about the room. 'It's quiet,' she said. 'Damned quiet. And you're quiet too. It's like living with wool in your ears. I'd be sick of it in a week. But I like your face. Give me a kiss.'

I kissed her once and even twice. She was no more emotional about that than about anything else. She sighed again, powdered her nose, and looked out of the window once more.

Then, as though she'd thought it out, turning to me she said:

'If Mulligan won't listen, ask him if he remembers 39 Lester Road. And if he doesn't listen to that, remind him of Mrs Bradley and the Four-

In-Hand Pub. If he wants more than that, say that you've got Ted Roscoe's address, and if *that* doesn't cool his fever come to me for it.'

I wrote this information down.

'Is this going to get you into any trouble?' I asked her.

'None that matters,' she answered indifferently. 'Mulligan doesn't dare touch me, and no one else can do anything. Besides, I'm past being hurt.'

'It's most awfully good of you,' I began fatuously.

'Damn manners,' she answered. 'I like your face and I've a sort of weakness for that Rossett boy. He's so bloody weakminded.'

She shook hands with me like a duchess. I went with her to the door.

'Wish I could get really interested in something again,' she said. 'You were something for a week or two, but now I've seen the way you live I know I couldn't stand it – Ta-ta.'

I saw Jean twice yesterday. I've told her nothing of my adventures and naturally her brother doesn't confide in her. But she knows that I'm after something and has a trust in me that shames me. I've become suddenly everything to her. She's never had anyone in her life before who cared for her more than for anyone else. Nor have I when it comes to that.

And it's glorious.

Greetings to Marjorie. Don't move out of bed a moment before you should. Love to old Rossett.

Affectionately,
MARK.

                                              PINE HOUSE,
                                              LAMBDALE.
MY DEAR MARK,

   Many thanks for all your strange news. It's good to know that you and
Jean are so happy together. Never mind what she says about not being
able to marry. We'll see to that. And I'm sure you'll get that young idiot
of a brother out of the soup, the mulligatawny. But what a queer world
you have had to dive into! It's like lifting a stone and looking underneath.
You are being a tremendous hero and, I have no doubt, are really
enjoying it immensely.

   As you see, we are still under Mrs Masham's roof; I can just hobble
about now. Rossett went home the day before yesterday, but is coming
as often as the car will fetch him. Marjorie, who is now deep in my
plot and is a far more artful Much Ado-er About Nothing (think that
over) than I am, has been playing the old fellow very cunningly. He
gives her great entertainment. Mrs Masham – of whom, to be frank,
she is very tired – she leaves to me. We had a long chat this very
morning. She is a simple old creature, really, and so long as I can keep
her away from prophecies and revelations and the infinite and the
superconscious (and her attachment to these things is by no means so
strong as it was), I find her quite amusing. She's very self-centred but
kindly disposed towards a world she certainly has not begun to
understand.

   She was very troubled this morning because she had just learned that
her favourite nephew (do you remember my telling you about him? – a
young ass who talked about nothing but the Riviera) has become
dreadfully entangled with a Russian female, twice his age, at Nice.
'Simply a notorious woman, I do assure you, Mr Newlands,' she told me.
'It's all very unconventional, but I don't mind that; I'm not a
conventional woman; I believe that the mighty force of Love should
never be chained by the conventions; but I know she will drag him
down, will prey upon him, keep him earth-bound. It's a tragic
disappointment to me, for I've done so much to raise him.'

   'Earth-bound, eh?' I said. 'Let me see. Isn't that what you called
Rossett? I meant to tell him that, but I never did. I couldn't have done,
of course, after what he said to me about you.' I looked her in the eye
and noticed signs of confusion.

'Earth-bound in a different sense,' she protested. Then she admitted that she might have used the term in a lower sense at first, when she didn't know him so well, and really it was strange – or would appear strange to those who did not peer below the surface of this life – that she should have used it at all, for in its higher sense it was true of him. 'A real lover of the soil,' she called him now; one of those whose vocation it is to guard the very earth itself; and a strong aristocratic soul. In other words, though I didn't present her with 'em, he was a fine figure of an old gentleman, and now she had her eye on him.

I was emboldened to ask her if he had given her any advice about buying land. I told her how troubled he had been, apparently for her sake, when I had mentioned it to him.

Yes, he had mentioned it, the very morning, that dreadful morning we climbed the mountain, and she had told him how glad she would be of his assistance. Nothing more had been said since. 'Really we've all been too busy,' she went on, 'what with your ankle and one thing and another. And you and Marjorie making up your little differences. Oh, I've seen it all. Quite a romance!' And she smirked at me and then gave a huge sigh, that of one who was finding the higher realms of thought and being a little chill or arid.

'I see that you have changed your opinion about Mr Rossett,' I observed, 'and that you now agree with what I first told you.' My voice invited confidences.

'Well, he let slip something the other day,' she said, 'that touched me, especially as coming from that proud nature. He let slip that he was lonely. That touched me.'

'Can you keep a secret?' I asked. Then I told her that Rossett would probably be lonelier still very soon, because his daughter would be marrying a friend of mine, whom she had met here. The son too would probably not come back.

'Dear, dear, dear,' she murmured, shedding the higher thinker and turning more and more into a rather simple middle-aged woman with every word. 'He will be lonely here, won't he? Ah, and I know what it means. You mightn't think I had been lonely, with my work and all my friends and so much money, too, but somehow I have been. As you get older, you get lonelier. And now for years I haven't had what you might call a fixed centre, a changeless haven on this earth. But I mustn't talk like this or I shall be falling in your estimation, shan't I, a woman with my advanced views?'

I didn't tell her that she never stood higher in my estimation than she did at that moment, but I looked very sympathetic. Then suddenly I pretended to be bright and ruthless. 'You know, if you wanted Farthing Hall and the old estate there, I believe it could be yours to-morrow.'

'What d'you mean?' she gasped.

'I mean that you could buy it as easily as that.' And I snapped my fingers and watched her face fall. 'It's all mortgaged. Rossett's poor now, very poor. You could buy him out, turn him off, without inconveniencing yourself. After all, they've been there long enough, these Rossetts.'

'I should never dream of doing such a thing. The very idea! Poor Mr Rossett!' She was very indignant. 'I should never pass one comfortable night in the house after doing a thing like that. Such a distinguished old family too, one of our very best!'

Yes, I said, very good blood there. Nevertheless it wouldn't be long before somebody would be turning them out, I assured her. Only a matter of months. Everything would have to go. Had she seen the lovely old treasures of the house?

No, she had not. At that moment Marjorie came in, and I told her in a loud voice crammed with meaning that Mrs Masham had never examined the treasures of Farthing Hall.

'How funny you should have said that!' cried Marjorie, producing a letter and holding it out for our inspection. It was from Rossett, asking us all three to dine with him to-morrow night. Everything, I believe, hangs on to-morrow night, and Farthing Hall – and rightly when you come to think of it – shall be our Trafalgar. Clean up the mess at your end and then wait for the postman.

Yours,
ROBERT.

P.S. – I have just been examining Rossett's note. What sort of a fist does he write? You know at once, don't you? – huge sprawling letters, thick strokes, stabs of the pen, and so forth. Well, as a matter of fact, he writes a very neat, small, graceful, feminine hand, like somebody in *Persuasion*. That's the kind of world it is – odd as a jelly-fish.

20 JERMYN STREET.

MY DEAR BOB,

A few days back you wrote me the longest letter of your life. I repeat
the compliment by now writing you the longest of mine – the longest I
shall ever write to any human being save Jean, and she is not really to be
excepted because I mean, once we are married, never to be separated
from her for twenty-four hours again.

This will be a long letter because I think it writes Climax and Finale to
the whole of my adventure. There are one or two little things still to be
cleared up – Jean must for instance break off her ridiculous engagement
with the gentleman up north, and something, the Lord knows what, has
got to be done about old man Rossett, but the events of two hours ago (I
am writing this letter in my own room – it is just after midnight) do set a
seal on my 'Uncle Silas' cum 'Dracula' existence. You shall hear.

The last days have been very difficult. Young Rossett has, for one
thing, been a great trouble. He is breaking down under Mulligan's
treatment of him. I got quite clearly from him yesterday that he forged
last year two papers in order to obtain possession of some property that
he proposed to sell to some other party – and did sell eventually.
Mulligan has the papers. He was also in some very unpleasant game of
Mulligan's, and was the catspaw of the party – some gambling game, I
gathered. He protests that he is completely and utterly sick of the whole
business. Whether it's only a matter of 'The Devil was sick', I don't
know, but I fancy that there is something decent in the fellow – how
could there not be and he Jean's brother? If only some strong-minded
woman would take him in hand! But where's the woman would be
bothered with such a creature?

I tried to persuade him that Mulligan is not such a terror as he
imagines, that he's only a dirty bladder of a bully to be pricked easily
enough, but two forged documents are pretty concrete things, and last
night he sat on my dingy sofa and bedewed it with his hot tears.

He seems to be able to do nothing now but cry. His nerve is really
now quite completely gone; or was until the marvellous events of this
evening of which I am going to tell you.

But there is in any case this much decent about him. He hates the idea
of jail, of course – that's natural enough – but worse than that to him is
the shock that the scandal would be to his father's family pride. He hates

the old man but respects that in him; not for himself, of course – he says repeatedly that he wishes he'd never had any family – but he has just imagination enough to realise that that passion in his father is a *big* passion, something larger and finer than anything that he has in himself.

My other difficulty has been with Jean. She has, during the last days, been working herself into a frantic state over her brother. He will tell her nothing, and to do him justice he has tried to pull himself together when he is with her. But she knows him well enough to realise that he is in bad fear of something or somebody, and being in the dark makes it, of course, all the harder for her.

I haven't been able to tell her anything either except that she must trust me, that I'm confident I'm going to pull the thing through – which, until to-night, God knows I wasn't. But her pluck and her courage are the finest of their kind. I've told you that she's old-fashioned – you've seen it yourself. She's got old ideas, old manners, old beliefs, and all I can say is that they stand her in such marvellous stead that if the much vaunted modern ones are as good I take off my hat to them.

Nevertheless she's desperate with anxiety. I have this at least to comfort myself with – that if I weren't beside her she'd do some rash, crazy, plucky thing that would probably put both herself and her brother into some fatal mess. She's as brave as Mussolini. I can imagine that to your modern cocktail-swilling Eton-cropped heroine she'd seem a nincompoop. She has never heard of Freud, never read a line of Aldous Huxley, and is intimate with none of the family of M. Charlus. I suit her and she suits me.

She is, I must add, scarcely aware of the existence of our friend Mr Mulligan – or wasn't until to-night. She'd met him twice, and he made no impression on her at all. He's simply a friend of her brother's who has been kind to that young hopeful, and so she's grateful to him. Or she was so until to-night. I think she realises him better now.

So to the tale. It was arranged after a lot of discussion that I should meet Mulligan this evening in Rossett's rooms. It was further arranged that Mulligan should bring the two forged documents with him. He was quite agreeable to this and said that he didn't mind in the least who saw them so long as Rossett didn't. It was the boy's affair. Only, he added, he wouldn't have supposed that Rossett would want more people to see them than was necessary.

His curiosity was piqued, I fancy. He couldn't imagine what exactly it was that I had up my sleeve. He supposed, I think, that I would offer a large sum of money for them, and although he had denied to me that he wanted money, still, if the sum offered were large enough, well, perhaps he would consider it. And then there was always the figure of Jean in the background.

We were to meet in Rossett's room in Glebe Place, Chelsea, at nine-thirty.

Well, a little in advance of time I went there. You know Glebe Place, of course, a fat rather self-satisfied little street directly off the King's Road, with studios on the one side of it and little houses greedy for lodgers on the other, and at the end of it a rustic cottage that looks as though Carlyle had contemptuously knocked his pipe against its walls – the kind of cottage he would greatly despise.

I rang a bell, was shown by a mutton-faced landlady up some shabby stairs and introduced to Rossett's room. Then I jumped with surprise. Do you remember my telling you in a letter once of a dream that I had, of my being with someone in a room, dusty and dishevelled old furniture, papers lying about and, of all things in the world, a harp standing in the corner? Well, believe it or believe it not, this was the very room. There could be no mistake, and I felt at once an odd musty sense of discomfort, a longing at once to back out and get away. I stared at the shabby harp and said to young Rossett, who got up eagerly as I came in:

'What's that thing doing here?' But he was in no mind to think of harps. He didn't even answer my question. 'Is it going to be all right?' he asked. 'Are you sure you can pull it off?'

I told him to go. I didn't want him there during the interview; he might, and probably would, spoil everything, his state being what it was. He went at once; he was obeying me then like a man mesmerised. I was, you see, his only hope.

So I was left alone there, and I tell you, Bob, I didn't half like it. All imagination of course. You've been to Farthing Hall and seen nothing either in it or its owner but geniality and pleasantness. But both there and in this other dirty room I have been conscious of the past. I'm not given to that; I'm not psychic or spooky; and you will probably say too that I'm wasting a lot of good time when I ought to be getting on with the real event by telling you about it. But there it is. The atmosphere of these two places has seemed in some kind of way to be more significant to me than anything else in my little story. It's true that the core of this adventure has been my love for Jean, but beyond it I have touched a world – a world of feeling and behaviour and unhappiness and frustration – that had never come near me before. It has changed me fundamentally. I know now how risky one's acts can be, and that there is no end to their consequences.

This room stank with past history. I opened the chattering window, tried to get the smell out of my nostrils. I touched the strings of the harp, and the dismal little sound was malevolent and actively revengeful. I was just wondering where Mulligan could be, and almost longing for him to break my isolation, when who do you think came in? Who but Jean herself!

She didn't, of course, know that I would be there. She cried out with surprise when she saw me. I was tempted to warn her back with my hand as though with every step that she took she was advancing into danger. Instead of that I took her in my arms and kissed her.

Then I told her: 'You've got to go.'

'Go?' she asked.

'At once.'

She looked at me with sharp suspicion.

'You're waiting for someone. You're in danger. I'm going to stay.'

I told her that I wasn't in any kind of danger. I was here on her brother's affairs, and she must leave me to carry it through.

A moment later she caught my hand. 'There's someone listening on the other side of the door,' she said. For a moment we were both terrified. It was the silliest thing. She couldn't possibly have heard anything, but I had the oddest sense that all the nasty furniture, the dingy sideboard, the rickety chairs, the dusty harp crowded in upon us as though they were trying to prevent our exit.

Then I broke the spell. I went to the door and opened it – and there, of course, on the other side was Mulligan.

He was very elegantly dressed, his bowler a little cocked. He seems to specialise in white waistcoats and buttonholes. He came casually forward, then saw Jean. His happy astonishment was splendid. He hadn't, of course, dreamt that she would be there. Whatever he had intended before to do or say, it was all forgotten now in his pleasure. He supposed, perhaps, that I had brought her there to make some kind of a bargain. In any case, he disregarded me entirely and moved towards her holding out his hand. But the look that he was giving her was enough for her. No man had ever looked at her like that before. In her fright she stepped back against me, and at once, without glancing at her, I took her to the door and out to the stairs.

She said nothing. She knew now that I would manage this better without her. I went back into the room, closing the door behind me.

'Well, Mr French,' he said. He was furious at my action. He looked for a moment as though he would brush past me to the door, but he thought better of it and stayed where he was. 'I haven't much time,' he said, 'I'm a busy man.'

'So am I,' I answered quite falsely.

I drew a chair to the rickety table and he stood, his legs spread, his hands in his pockets, glowering at me. We manoeuvred then for a little. I can't remember all that we said; we both talked a good deal. His point was that he had little time to spare, that this was all nonsense anyway, but that he was a good-natured fellow and would like to help his young friend Rossett. I replied that the best way to help his young friend was to leave him alone, and that if he would promise me that and would hand over the two papers, our little talk was over. He produced the two papers and gallantly allowed me to look at them – a dirty soiled pair of documents they were. The signatures, I was given to understand, were forgeries. Rossett had described them to me. I was sure that they were the goods, but in any case, if they weren't, it didn't much matter. Either I had enough power over Mulligan or I hadn't. The rest followed.

At first it seemed that I hadn't. The man was supremely confident, with all the brass in the world. He made up his mind that I was no danger to him and, after that, rather liked me, I think. We became suddenly rather friendly. He took a chair and drew it close to mine. I asked him whether he still meant what he had said the other night, that money was nothing to him. I said five hundred. He laughed. I said a thousand. He said he might do something for five thousand.

He came closer. He even put his hand on my shoulder.

'Look here,' he said, 'I like you. We might be pals. I could put you on to lots of things. Why not consider it?'

I moved away and, still very friendly, said that I didn't think we'd suit and that anyway I hadn't any money, and in addition to that, what about 39 Lester Road?

That was the moment of my danger. I believe that as he turned his gaze full on me, and stiffened his stout body against the little chair, I was as near death as I'm ever likely to be. What kind of death I don't know. As I spoke, he had stopped jingling the coins in his pocket. There may have been a revolver there or a neat little bludgeon or just a handkerchief. Who knows their ways? I certainly don't. Of one thing I am sure, that a man like Mulligan goes nowhere alone without some kind of weapon.

I believe too that in that second of time all the alternatives passed through his mind, many more alternatives than I was aware of, but that my silent and expeditious decease was one of them I am certain. I saw his watch gleam on his wrist as he turned his arm mechanically to look at it. His eyes, looking into mine, were as cold as pebbles. His hand moved ever so slightly towards me. I seemed to catch on my cheek his breath and it was as chilly as the room was stifling. I couldn't move; whatever he wanted to do he could have done with the greatest of ease.

This was no imagination, Bob, it was as real and vivid as the truest of nightmares. I smelt the scent of some meat that someone was roasting in a room beneath the open window. I remember thinking to myself, 'That's the last smell you'll ever smell.'

Well, he thought better of it. Too much risk, I suppose. Very friendly, he said:

'What do you know about Lester Road?'

'Ah, that would be telling,' I answered (my voice trembled a fraction in spite of myself), 'But this you can be sure of. Give me those two papers and I shan't bother you.'

He tried then to cover his admission. He said that he'd never heard of Lester Road and so on.

I let him talk for a bit and then I said: 'Well then – what about Mrs Bradley? And what about the Four-in-Hand Pub?'

After that he didn't try another thing. He got up and walked about the room. I sat quiet. He longed to finish me, I know. I could see him telling himself that he could do it so easily and so quietly, that no one would ever hear or know or bother – but in fact he went, I think, very quickly beyond me to his own particular case.

I heard him mutter as he swung round on his heel:

'That's the third since August.' He stood at the table looking at me.

'Here you are,' he said, very friendly, handing me the papers. 'The boy's a small affair after all.' Then, looking at me very steadily: 'This is between us – if I don't bother that young fool?'

'On my honour,' I answered.

'I believe you,' he said simply. 'And that's more than I'd do with most of my friends.' Then he added casually: 'There are too many know too much in this damned country. I think I'll try Canada for a bit.'

Then he said a funny thing. 'If you're ever after the goods, young man, give grape-fruit a miss. It's sour on the stomach. That was my mistake. I didn't consider my stomach enough.' He looked round the room, went up to the harp and touched the strings.

'Old-fashioned thing, a harp,' he said. 'So long,' and went.

Oh Lord! It's three-thirty! I've been living it all again. I'm shaking, whether with sleep or nerves I don't know.

But grape-fruit, Bob? Shall I ever eat them with comfort again?

That's all for the moment.

Your loving
MARK.

FARTHING HALL,
GARROWDALE.

MY DEAR MARK,

There's just time to catch the morning post with this. Doesn't this address make you stare? Rossett and Mrs Masham are engaged, yes, engaged, and very shortly to be married. It all happened last night, and you shall hear all about it as soon as I have time to write a proper letter. In the meantime, you can go ahead. Your troubles are over, thanks, in part, to your Machiavellian friend,

ROBERT.

FARTHING HALL,
GARROWDALE.

MY DEAR MARK,

Now for an account of last night. But don't expect a clear and concise narrative: you will have to wait for that until you see me. I'm still too muddled. Besides, I'm writing this in the breakfast-room of Farthing Hall (I'll bet you never knew it had one), to be out of people's way. I can't tell the story under the victims' noses, so I crept in here. But there's no fire here and I shouldn't think the room had been used for twenty years. It's all musty and queer, but at the same time devilish cold. And a man with a colossal nose, labelled Eglinton Rossett, Esquire, jeers at me from the opposite wall.

The shortest and therefore best way of doing it (I want to get back to the fire) is to divide it up into scenes. Scene One, then, is yesterday afternoon at Mrs Masham's. Merrow, the chauffeur, is tinkering with the car. I hobble out with a pipe and ask him what he is doing. It's this 'ere 'mag.,' he says; can't get 'er to start and knows it's the 'mag.' Fishes out the magneto, sees what it is wrong, tells me all about it, shows me that a screw – something to do with a contact-breaker – has come loose. I look on amiably, puffing at my pipe, but make a note of that screw.

Scene Two is the dining-room of Farthing Hall, last night. The kitchen has done its best, the cellar has done even better. Rossett has brought up his last treasures of liquor and is busy sampling them and pressing them upon his three guests. I drink heartily and muse wickedly. Mrs Masham – who could be compared to an Indian summer day – is rosy and magnificent and does not disdain the grape. Marjorie delicately sips and sparkles. After dinner we are shown the heirlooms. Rossett is immense, the great-uncle of Clio herself. But I have seen the heirlooms before, and so has Marjorie, who begs to be left alone with the miniatures. Rossett has Mrs Masham to himself, and her eye and ear wait upon him. Everything is as it should be, except that Time – the old enemy – is defeating us. He is slipping away, and there are the conventions, the proprieties, to be observed. Mrs Masham, as gigantically flushed as a sunset and yet demure – yes, demure – murmurs something about the time. This is in the hall. Marjorie is not stirring from her fire and miniatures. I do not demur about the time, but promise to limp across to the Brown Bull and see about the car.

Scene Three is in that open shed just outside the Brown Bull. The car is in that shed, and Merrow is in the Brown Bull, testing Trump's bottled beer. I creep into the shed, fish out an electric torch, and do not find it very difficult to remove a certain screw, quite a tiny little thing. (I will make you a present of it when you are married.) Then I make all safe, and loudly enter the Brown Bull, demanding Merrow. Mrs Masham wants the car. I even follow Merrow, in my easy friendly fashion, to watch him start the car. But no, 'e can't make 'er budge. He tries this and that, then tackles his 'mag.' Would you believe it, that 'ere screw clean gone, must 'ave loosed and then dropped out as we came along. It must be somewhere inside. May take some time to find it, but it must be there somewhere. I offer to take a message across to his employer. I find Mrs Masham and Rossett back in the dining-room, alone, and with their heads close together over a large volume, which I have no doubt had some reference to the famous old Rossetts. I suspect that her face falls when she sees me, nor does she show any impatience when I announce that Merrow is unable to start the car. I am told that Marjorie has fallen asleep in the drawing-room and that it would be a shame to disturb the poor darling, still so tired after all the excitement of the last few days. A shame indeed! I remark that I shall return to Merrow, who will, no doubt, be glad of my assistance. In reply to Rossett, who says that no doubt the fellow could do with a drink, I remark that no doubt he could. So we 'no doubted' one another, and I crept away.

The next scene is the same dining-room but later, much later. I have found Merrow in despair. 'E's looked and looked and better looked but can't find that – beggin' your pardon – something-something screw; and 'e's absolutely done. There's no shifting that car without the screw, and nothing to be done about it at that time of night. Never been in such a fix since he first went on the road. I'll bear witness that it's not his fault. Didn't I see him tighten that screw before we left? Will I take the message and try and make it all right for him with Mrs Masham? Yes, I will, like the good kind gentleman I am, and promise too that it *will* be all right. We shall have to stay here all night, and he had better find quarters for himself at the Brown Bull. Off he goes to knock up the Trumps, while I enter the dining-room of Farthing Hall once more. I find two people sitting over the fire, and they look up startled when I enter. I give them no time to say anything, but explain at once that the car is useless, and that we must all stay the night. They look at one another questioningly and then achieve a confused smile. Fortunately, I hear Mrs Masham murmur, she has a chaperone in Marjorie. Rossett rises, steps forward, puts out his chest, clears his throat, and then announces that Mrs Masham has just promised to be his wife. I am pleased but surprised, which delights the pair of them. I say that I must tell Marjorie at once and go to the drawing-room, only to find that this time she really is asleep. It seems ages since I saw her like that, sitting there in the fire-light. A kiss wakens her, and slowly and smilingly she drinks in the news. Then Rossett himself appears with the largest tray I have ever seen, and insists upon us all drinking in the news. Curtain.

We shall probably be here for several days. Mrs Masham is busy now getting rid of any traces of higher thought, and has already assumed the air of a chatelaine. She spent the greater part of this afternoon dragging Marjorie round this ancient mansion, altering this and putting in that in tremendous whispers. At tea she corrected us about some heirloom or other, and I'm sure that in a day or two all this array of relics and family treasures will be securely wedged in her own past. Every time she looks at anything here she seems to have known it ten years longer.

But isn't this splendid news for you? Write to me here, settle your fantastic affairs, and let us see you as soon as possible.

Yours,
ROBERT.

20 JERMYN STREET.

MY DEAR OLD BOB,

Hurray! Hurray! Hurray! – and Hurrah! Hurrah! Hurrah! At your Masham-Rossett news I laughed, I cried, I shouted, I danced.

Your letter came as I was splashing about in the last spot of marmalade and preparing to meet Jean and her brother just outside Spinks's shop. For a long time after I couldn't bother about any of your detail. I just shoved the letter into my pocket, wiped the marmalade off my mouth, and rushed into Spinks's. I was far too early, of course, and I stood there tattooing with my feet, staring into the eyes of Egyptian gods and goddesses, appraising ropes of amber and pearl, watching old connoisseurs totter up the steps of Christie's, gaily winking at a school of pigeons doing French exercises on a roof-ledge on the opposite side of the street – and all the time my heart or my pancreas or my liver (maybe all three together) was singing 'Bob's spliced Masham and Rossett – Bob's spliced Masham and Rossett – and Jean and I are free – Jean and I are FREE! – Jean and I are FREE!'

A moment later they both turned up and *what* news I had for them. First, safe from Mulligan, second, father disposed of, and third! Third – Oh, well, what did we all do but hurry into Christie's as though we were about to buy a Thirty Thousand Romney and were afraid someone else was ahead of us. Once in there among an untidy collection of ghostly furniture and sad neglected pictures, we all sat down on a sofa (upon which I'm sure we had no right whatever to sit) and rattled out our news. I'm sure Christie's has never in all its glorious history witnessed a happier scene. Indeed a Queen Anne bureau with the most heavenly intricate beauties about its drawers and legs simply trembled with pleasure as it watched us. It had been having the dreariest time for days.

Of course young Rossett's a scoundrel, a wastrel, and a ne'er-do-well. I had his dirty forged documents in my pocket as we were talking (I wasn't, of course, going to let Jean have a look at them or even know of their existence). But I must confess that there on that old sofa opposite the Queen Anne bureau with its beauty and tolerance and sense of the fine charity of passing time I couldn't feel much severity.

To see that fear and anxiety lift from the boy's face was a good sight, let him have done what he may.

We alluded very vaguely to the documents because of Jean's presence, but he understood enough to know that they were safe in my keeping and before the end of that day would be ashes in the fire.

And I gave my old friend Dora Mellin the credit. Why not? She may do something for the young ass yet. They could do worse than marry. At least he would not beat her. In fact I'm certain that she would wear the trousers – enough to stiffen his poor wobbly character a bit anyway.

And then, hugging my luxury as long as I might, I told the two of them and the Queen Anne bureau my other great piece of news – *your* other great piece of news.

At first they simply refused to credit it. That *anyone* should have pluck and optimism enough to marry their father. But the Queen Anne bureau confirmed my statement – told them in fact that it had seen far stranger things in *its* time, nodded its pretty head in the sagest, most fatherly manner.

So they believed it, and Jean then and there, before all the pictures (most of the furniture was asleep and didn't notice) kissed me twice.

Then I heard her sigh – she was lifting away from her all that burden of responsibility that had been for years weighing her down.

Poor child! Darling, darling child! In another few days you shall see both of us – and, best friend that man has ever had, shall bless us both.

Your loving
MARK.

FARTHING HALL,
GARROWDALE.

MY DEAR MARK,

Exit the villain then. Your letters are our only reading. Marjorie flatly
refuses to believe a word of them, says that you and Jean go walking
about London hand-in-hand, making it all up. I refute her with Farthing
Hall. She has to believe in this place, you see, for she contrives to eat and
drink and sleep in it. We have the largest bedroom in Cumberland; it
goes on and on, and then turns a corner. Our colossal four-poster is at
the other end, and when you climb into it you watch that dusky and
distant corner all the time, for anything might come round it. The whole
room, indeed, is slightly crazy, and all the portraits on the walls (and the
Rossetts seem to have liked nothing better than giving bad portrait
painters innumerable commissions) are of people who are obviously in
the know about the room and are keeping their eye on you all the time
to see how you will like *It* when *It* comes. Marjorie says that every time
she does her hair the room comes crowding round her, corner and all.
The enormous wardrobe clearly contains a huddle of old corpses, and so
we never open its doors. There are very few hooks and things, and what
there are Marjorie claims, so every night I hang my coat over a rusted
antique musket. So much for Farthing Hall.

The news of Rossett's impending marriage has excited the whole dale.
There is only one person who is aggrieved and that is your old friend
Trump. 'No, Mr Newlands,' he told me, 'I don't like it. It's a defection,
that's what it is, a defection. I've had talk, as you know, with Mrs
Masham, and though I don't say she was altogether sound – a bit
superstitious and fantastic, you might say – she was on the way, sir. Yes,
she was on the way. A Mind was there. If she'd gone on, she might have
turned out a Friend to Humanity. And that's better than being the third
Mrs Rossett. But you see what it is, she gives in, takes the line of least
resistance. That's our trouble now, sir, that is – line of least resistance.
Look at these Fassistis.' Good old Trump! I left him looking
disapprovingly at the Fascisti.

I keep my eye on Rossett, though he spends a good deal of his time in
a strange little cubby-hole, where he can hardly move for documents,
walking-sticks, guns, boots and leggings, and empty tobacco tins. There
he labours, I fancy, to discover in what sort of tangle his affairs are, but

his marriage will have come and gone long before he succeeds. I keep my eye on him, though, because I cannot help wondering what will happen to him once he is married. It will be one of two extremes: either he will be drunker and more arrogant and absurd than he ever was before; or he will be very quickly sobered, cleaned, tamed, bitted and bridled. You will be probably surprised to learn that I am ready to offer odds of two to one on a tamed Rossett. But then I have noticed a certain speculative look that Mrs Masham sometimes turns upon him; and Marjorie tells me that she is by no means so foolish as she seems, having brought character out of her long-past battles with this life, and being particularly shrewd where money is concerned. But this is no way to talk about your future father-in-law and mother-in-law.

My dear lad, I am longing to see you again; if you stay away much longer and I write to you much more, I shall cease to believe in your real existence. I look forward to a glorious day or two's yarning over all these antics of the autumn, and I also look forward to being free of the necessity of writing to you, Special Correspondent fashion, every other day. A friend's a fellow you can talk with, letting the words tumble out anyhow, pell-mell, and writing is only for creatures – very pleasant creatures, of course – called Readers. Curiously enough, I am becoming interested in them again, and feel an itch to try and piece together that *Chimera of Romanticism*. Yes, I know I swore off it, but the work's there to hand – and 'why, Hal, 'tis my vocation, Hal; 'tis no sin for a man to labour in his vocation.' Besides, Marjorie, who gave me the impression before that she disliked the thing, told me last night that the second chapter is the best piece of writing I have ever done.

And you must come, bringing your shy beauty home, and when you have kissed and shaken hands and told your tale all round, get out your sketch-book and set down once and for all this countryside and these marvellous mornings we are having now. This morning Marjorie and I strolled up the dale and almost thought ourselves bewitched, it was so beautiful. Your three crinkly hills were like bubbles of green and grey, hanging against the sky; a breath would have floated them away; and the whole dale looked as if it had newly come from the mint. Only the Hall was old, older by far than the twisted veins of rock and the long slopes in the sunlight. But you will see for yourself. Come down and work before the light goes.

And I swear that you will have nothing from me for the rest of our days but post cards and telegrams.

Yours,
ROBERT.

20 JERMYN STREET.

DEAR BOB,

Your letter that came in by the afternoon post was a farewell – not to myself, thank goodness, but to all this episode of ours, this correspondence, this 'Midsummer Night's Dream,' this 'Northanger Abbey' fantasy. You return to Marjorie and your *Chimera*, I begin my real life with Jean at my side and an almost drunken longing for my paint-brushes such as I've never before known. In another week's time all of us together at Farthing Hall will doubt the reality of it. I am glad that at least we have the letters to amuse us in our old age.

I was asleep in front of the fire just now – or was I? Anyway I moved in a jumbled world where trees were made of marzipan, streams of crystal, and Farthing Hall spawned ridiculous ghosts, all broomstick and blanket with turnip-lanterns for heads. And there were yourself and Marjorie and the Masham and Rossett and Mulligan and Dora Mellin and Trump and the old man who so long ago in the hotel at Keswick dropped stamps on the floor and called on the Deity. Then suddenly in the middle of them was the White Rabbit, hurrying along looking for his glove, and the cook throwing pepper at the Duchess and the Queen shouting, 'Off with his head!' and the Walrus and the Carpenter stepping along the shining sands, the oysters following dutifully after.

I loved you all. I embraced the world in an ecstasy of charity, and the Queen, having just condemned a dozen of her courtiers to death, remarked, 'If only they'd take Epsom Salts in the morning they wouldn't mind half so much.' Upon which Mulligan, chief executioner to the Queen, added very respectfully:

'It's grape-fruit, your Majesty, that's the ruin of most of them.'

I may tell you that young Rossett thinks Dora Mellin, his recent rescuer, the finest woman in the world – and is there room at Farthing Hall for Jean and myself? – and has Father Rossett forgiven me?

Yours,

MARK.

Telegram from
   ROBERT NEWLANDS
to
   MARK FRENCH.

Catch ten-thirty Keswick will meet you.

ROBERT.

Telegram from
   MARK FRENCH.
to
   ROBERT NEWLANDS.

Are catching ten-thirty Keswick.

MARK. JEAN.

JUDITH PARIS

HUGH WALPOLE

'The canvas is huge, but something is happening; there is movement, colour, life, in every square inch of it. There is not one tired, listless page. The tale is bewilderingly opulent; the mountains stand up in the sun, mist and rain; crowds gather to hoot and yell or to eat and drink and tumble one another; characters by the score come and go, and nearly all of them leap to the eye at once.'   J. B. PRIESTLEY

The Herries Chronicle is the rich and romantic history of an English Lake District family from 1730 to 1932. The story of Judith Paris, which may be enjoyed without any knowledge of her forebears or her descendants, is both warm and tragic. An impetuous and passionate character, with enormous strength of spirit, she arouses feelings of both tenderness and despair in those around her. Curious about love and determined to make something of her life, she excites also the passions of two very different men: the sturdy, affectionate Reuben, her half-cousin; and Georges Paris, a Frenchman, whose wilful and dangerous nature seems to respond to her own. Set against a background of the French Revolution, the story of Judith Paris is alternately amusing, violent and touching.

THE FORTRESS

HUGH WALPOLE

'It had been the wish of her whole life to flee from all the
Herries but Walter Herries had challenged her and she had
taken up the challenge.' Judith Paris, now nearing fifty,
returns to the Lakes to confront the bitter feud between the
two branches of the Herries family. Walter, now living in
Westaways, and as powerful as he is determined, wants to own
Fell House, which once belonged to his father, but which is
now home to the defenceless Jennifer and her children. To
this end he ensures that everything Jennifer plans to improve
her situation meets with failure, and he begins to build the
huge house known as The Fortress which will overshadow
her land. His one weakness is his children, whom he loves
with a fierce affection, but will they too be drawn into the
web of love and loss?

This third volume of the Herries Chronicles traces the
rich and romantic history of an English Lake District family
through fifty years – from the summer fair at Keswick to the
coronation of Queen Victoria.